My name is Callum Ormond.
I am fifteen
and I am a hunted fugitive . . .

CONSPIRACY 365

BOOK FOUR: APRIL

To Becks

First American Paperback Edition 2012
First American Edition 2010
Kane Miller, A Division of EDC Publishing

Text copyright © Gabrielle Lord, 2010
Cover design copyright © Scholastic Australia, 2010
Illustrations copyright © Scholastic Australia, 2010
Back cover photo of boy's face © Scholastic Australia, 2010
Cover photo of boy © Scholastic Australia, 2010
Cover design by Natalie Winter
Illustrations by Rebecca Young

First published by Scholastic Australia Pty Limited in 2010
This edition published under licence from Scholastic Australia Pty Limited

Library of Congress Control Number: 2009934760

Printed and bound in the United States of America
1 2 3 4 5 6 7 8 9 10
ISBN: 978-1-61067-106-4

BOOK FOUR: APRIL

GABRIELLE LORD

A DIVISION OF EDC PUBLISHING

PREVIOUSLY . . .

1 MARCH

I'm facing a gruesome death. The train is right in front of me, inches away, but just before impact I fall, somehow, through the tracks. Repro has saved me — a strange guy who trusts me with the location of his secret hideout.

4 MARCH

A newspaper article about my family shows Mum and Rafe pleading for me to come home. I fear my coma-stricken sister Gabbi must be deteriorating.

8 MARCH

Boges and I meet up and go through the drawings again. We realize I must go to Mount Helicon to see if Great-uncle Bartholomew can help with information.

11 MARCH

We find a clue in the photo I took of Oriana de la

Force. We can see part of a word, I-D-D-L-E, on her desk. I try calling Eric Blair, but I'm told he's still on sick leave.

18 MARCH
I finally meet Jennifer Smith in the laboratories of Labtech. She reveals that she has a memory stick that Dad wanted me to have — containing photos of fields and ruins from Ireland. Sligo's thugs suddenly interrupt us, and during their attack I crash into a glass case, releasing the death adders! Within seconds, one strikes at my leg, and I realize I don't have long before the poison kills me. In a sick haze, I manage to locate and inject the antivenom. As I recover, I find that Jennifer has been knocked out, but will be OK. I flee, knowing I'll have to get the memory stick from her another time.

25 MARCH
Boges and Winter don't exactly hit it off when they both show up at the St. Johns house. I'm told Rafe has hired a detective to look for me, and that Sligo's almost on to my hiding place. A riot cop stumbles straight into the house, chasing a thief. Winter disappears. A cop wrestles with Boges until I jab him with one of my tranquilizers.

Before we escape, I grab the pepper spray from his belt. Later that night, I see my double again.

30 MARCH
Repro and I sneak into Oriana's place and steal a folder containing the Ormond Riddle! Repro tackles Kelvin, allowing me to get away through the window and down the tree.

31 MARCH
I have the Riddle, and I'm on my way to Mount Helicon. I hitch a ride with a guy in a pickup truck. Lachlan, the driver, notices we're being followed by an SUV. Sumo and Kelvin are behind the wheel! They start ramming us. We're going nearly 120 miles an hour to avoid them when the monster truck bumps us a final time, and we lose control, flying over the embankment and rolling down into a shallow creek. Lachlan's alive, but pinned under his truck with his head underwater. I'm forced to stay and hold his head up so that he won't drown. I can already hear the thugs thrashing down through the bush. I can't leave Lachlan to die . . .

1 APRIL

275 days to go . . .

Blackwattle Creek

12:00 am

Closer and closer came the rustling of slow, careful footsteps. My exhausted body shrank further against the rock face I'd quickly hidden behind. A beam of light from a powerful flashlight cut through the darkness ahead, about ten yards away, shining through the trees and bushes I'd just run through. He was taking his time tracking me and wouldn't have needed a lot of skill to follow the mess I'd made, charging through the scrub recklessly with my backpack.

I'd been running nonstop since we crashed in Lachlan's truck down at the creek, a couple of hours ago now, but I was exhausted and had to stop for breath and hide. Everything was aching, and the impact of the seatbelt across my body had flared up the pain in my right shoulder again.

I stepped sideways and further behind the rocky outcrop, so that the flashlight was no longer visible. I felt around and found the opening to a sort of cleft, a split in the rocks. I squeezed myself into it, as deep as I could, until it became too narrow for me to go any further. Unless he shone the light directly into this crevice, I could remain unseen.

I waited. I listened. All I could hear was the blood pounding in my ears. Then there was another crackle of leaves. And another, as whoever was tailing me stealthily crept through the trees some distance away.

Another snapping of twigs as a heavy footfall crushed them . . .

I waited, too scared to breathe, as the sound of the footsteps became louder.

12:03 am

The unmistakable silhouette of the sumo wrestler — the guy I'd attacked with pepper spray back at Oriana de la Force's house — appeared in the moonlight. He paused almost directly in front of the cleft I was huddled in. I held my breath again. If he got his hands on me I was in all sorts of serious trouble. He and his mate Kelvin had tried to kill us by running us off the road in their monster truck, and now he'd followed me here, chased after me through endless masses of bushland to finish off the job.

He shone his flashlight around him without moving from his position. The beam of light slowly traveled over the damp scrub, fallen logs and the rocky wall I was hidden in. I closed my eyes. Surely he wouldn't miss me from where he was.

I opened them again. The beam of light climbed up and over the walls of the narrow cleft, coming closer and closer to me. Any moment now he'd see me squashed inside.

But the flashlight passed right over my head, completely missing me! Unbelievably, I hadn't been spotted!

12:12 am

Eventually he moved on through the bushes, the sound of his rustling movement slowly fading. I was weak with relief, but didn't dare let myself relax — not even for a second — in case he was still hanging around. As I pictured him creeping, searching out there, my mind started skipping back to the accident, replaying everything that had happened only a couple of hours ago . . . the terror of the high-speed chase on the highway, Oriana's thugs — Sumo and Kelvin — in their SUV, relentlessly charging us from behind . . . and then, finally, being rammed off the road completely . . . when Lachlan's pickup, with us trapped helplessly inside, rolled down the hill and crashed into the creek.

The silence that followed the crash had quickly filled with the sounds of the night — distant bird calls, far-off cattle, the drone of insects. We'd ended up about fifty yards down from the road, upturned and bogged in shallow water. I'd managed to climb out of the wreckage, but Lachlan — poor, innocent Lachlan Drysdale — was unconscious and completely pinned under his truck . . . I had no choice but to stay there crouched over him, holding his flopping head out of the water to stop him from drowning. There was no way I was going to leave him there alone to die.

My feet were sinking into the mud as I'd held him there, waiting for Oriana's thugs to thunder down the pulverized leaves and saplings and grab me.

And then the dreaded sound had come: someone running towards us. For a second I'd panicked and considered grabbing my backpack, with the Riddle in it, and letting Lachlan's head drop underwater . . . but I knew I could never do that, so I braced myself instead for the inevitable. I'd escaped from these people before, I told myself — I could do it again.

The bushes just above the creek parted, and my heart jumped in fear. But instead of Sumo or Kelvin pouncing on me, it was a tall police officer hurrying over to help!

"Are you OK?" he'd called out as he looked around, assessing the scene. "I saw what happened up there on the road. Where's the driver?"

"He's here," I'd said, gesturing to Lachlan with a nod of my head, while trying to keep my shaky voice under control and ignore the images of juvenile prison that were flashing through my mind. "He's breathing, but he's unconscious and pinned down. I just can't get him out. I've been holding his head out of the water . . . I've got a few scratches, but I'm fine."

"Your friend is very lucky you were here," the cop had said as he squatted down beside us, a frown drawing his fair eyebrows together, "otherwise . . . well, let's not think about that. I was chasing that crazy SUV that was tailgating you when I saw your vehicle fly over the embankment . . . Are you sure you're not hurt anywhere?"

"I'm fine," I said. "Nothing's broken."

"Here, let me take him." The cop then shifted into my position and took Lachlan's head from my hands. "I've radioed for an ambulance and rescue team, along with police backup. They'll be able to free your friend here, and get you checked out too. I reckon the highway patrol will have located the vehicle responsible for this by now."

I was finally free to stand up. I stretched out my arms and clenched and unclenched my aching fingers, sore from bearing the weight of Lachlan's head. While the cop had been talking, my mind had been racing in overdrive — desperately thinking of a way to get my stuff and get out of there. More cops were coming, and I knew that if I didn't run, I'd be recognized and cuffed in no time. *Psycho Kid*, public enemy number one . . . the guy who'd attacked his uncle and put his sister in a coma.

The sound of a thunderous explosion suddenly boomed down from the highway. The cop and I both instinctively ducked for cover, bracing ourselves. When we emerged, we stared, shocked, in the direction it had come from — a massive fireball shot up into the sky, followed by a mushroom cloud of billowing smoke.

The cop muttered and adjusted his shaky hold on Lachlan's head.

"I bet that was the SUV!" he said, fumbling with his free hand to grab his radio. "Those jerks had better not have collided with one of our squad cars!"

A siren wailed in the distance. I had to go. I knew Lachlan would be OK; I just hoped he wouldn't tell anyone that I was headed to Mount Helicon. For some reason, I felt pretty sure he wouldn't.

As soon as I'd reached into the cab of the pickup to grab my backpack, the cop had started shouting at me, asking me what I was doing. Without a word, I'd hitched my backpack high up on my shoulders and started scrambling away, leaving the pickup and the two figures behind me, one unconscious and one completely confused and shouting. I ran following the creek, crashing and falling over half-buried logs and timber and dodging dense scrub, not stopping for a good two hours, at least. The cop had no choice but to stay behind and keep Lachlan's head above water.

Even as I was running away I was thinking

I was doomed — I figured there'd be more cops and sniffer dogs on my trail in no time. I crossed a wide section of the creek a few miles down from the crash site, which I knew from watching so many action movies with Dad, meant the end of the dogs being able to track my scent. It also meant that now my jeans and sneakers were completely drenched.

The *dogs* had lost me maybe, but not Sumo. I was hidden in a rock, surely miles away from where we'd crashed in the creek, thinking that he and Kelvin probably perished in that highway explosion . . . and yet, somehow, he'd managed to almost find me in the dark middle of nowhere.

12:39 am

I'd just begun to cautiously squeeze out of my hiding place, keen to have a better look around, when from somewhere in the shadows came a sharp, cracking sound, followed by a squeak. Immediately, I jumped back into position — concealed, invisible and motionless. Had Sumo returned?

The squeaking became more desperate.

When heavy wings flapped overhead, I exhaled with relief. It was just a night bird catching its prey.

I started wondering again how Lachlan was and whether he was OK. By now he was probably sleeping and recovering in a quiet hospital bed somewhere. They must have known it was me that ran from the scene . . . The press would be hounding him in the morning for information. Everyone would be trying to get a big break, an exclusive story, on the teen fugitive. I was sure Lachlan would never pull over to offer a stranger a ride ever again.

Poor guy. I owed him, just like I owed Repro.

I didn't even know where Repro was, or how he'd managed to escape from Oriana's place after we stole the Riddle from her desk. I hoped he was safe with his collection, in his crazy little place hidden in the middle of the city. I wished I could be there with him, instead of being on the run in the depths of the bush. But right now, I had to deal with reality. It was time to move on.

12:48 am

A quarter moon shone over the ridge, and the wind stirred the surrounding treetops. Overhead, stars twinkled in a deep black sky. I figured Sumo must have been pretty far away from me by now, or better still, had given up searching for me altogether. But what about his partner, Kelvin? Maybe he'd been hurt in the fiery explosion up on the highway earlier. If not, would the two of them meet up and go back to the city, or would they continue hunting me here?

I decided it was safe enough to come out from the rock wall. I extricated myself from my squashed position, pulled on my backpack, and with every sense quivering, I cautiously continued my journey. I didn't have a clue where I was — all I knew was that I would have to be very careful and that I was a long, long way from the pickup truck.

The sound of crickets and insects buzzed in my ears, and beyond that I thought I could hear the hum of distant traffic — trucks on the highway perhaps. In spite of everything — the fact that I was completely lost in the scrub without hope of shelter or safety, and I was tired and hungry — I couldn't help feeling excited. Stashed in my backpack was what I hoped would be the key to the mystery that my dad had stumbled on. I'd finally gotten hold of the Ormond Riddle, and I couldn't wait to pull it out and have a good look at it.

1:19 am

The pale light of the moon had been some help earlier, but now it was hidden, and I was floundering around in the dark. I wasn't about to use my flashlight for fear of highlighting my position, so I blindly pushed on. My sneakers were still wet and squelching, my jeans soaked, and I kept knocking my shins painfully against rocks and branches that stuck out in the path I was making. A couple of times I stumbled, falling flat on my face.

I slowed for a moment to try and call Boges, but my phone had no signal at all. I was exhausted. I needed to stop for the night — make some sort of camp where I could feel safe enough to try and get some sleep. It felt like I'd done nothing but run for twenty-four hours.

If I could find a cave, I thought, where I could camouflage the entrance, I might be able to relax and get some shut-eye. With all these rocks around, surely there'd be some cave-like shelters, even if it was only some sort of big overhang.

I peered ahead into the darkness and spotted something unusual. Surprised, I took cover behind a clump of prickly bushes. Ahead of me in a small clearing was a very small house — kind of like a hut or a shed. Why would someone build something like this out in the middle of nowhere? There didn't seem to be anyone around. The place was in total darkness. Carefully, I approached, listening intently.

Something flapped past me, and I jumped back. Spooked, I crouched down, listening again.

When I was totally sure the hut was empty, I crept closer.

Sometimes there were cabins in the forests for bushwalkers and climbers, and I wondered if this was one of them. I'd heard that the rangers kept them stocked with firewood, matches, a water tank, an environmentally-friendly toilet, and basic supplies.

I walked all the way around the hut until I was almost back at the front again.

I had a drink from the rainwater tank that was attached to the hut's side and then very carefully checked the door. I turned the handle and went to open it. It was stiff, and I had to push hard against it, but eventually it opened right up.

As it did so, something bumped past my face, and I jumped back in fright! Then whatever it was flew off high above me. I looked up, but couldn't see anything. A bird or a bat must have been trapped in there. A cold wind suddenly blew up again, making an eerie sound in the treetops. I quickly stepped inside.

Digging around in my backpack, I found my flashlight, switched it on and shone it over the interior of the hut.

It was a really small space — not much bigger than my bedroom at home. It had a table in the center, a couple of benches on either side, some cots stacked in a corner, a stone fireplace against one wall with a mantle running along the top, a large box with rope handles, two old lamps hanging on hooks and several drums, one of which was marked, "Kerosene."

On the mantle, covered with dusty spider webs, rested several boxes.

I closed the door behind me, pulled my backpack off and slung it onto the wooden table, then collapsed onto a bench. I had some shelter. Finally, I could stop running — for a while.

2:02 am

The first thing I did, after getting back up and lighting a kerosene lamp, was pull out my supply of chocolate that I'd bought when Lachlan and I stopped at the gas station for sandwiches yesterday. After that, I opened my backpack and pulled out Oriana's folder containing the Ormond Riddle.

Carefully, I slid the Riddle out of its protective plastic sleeve. This was the first chance I'd had since stealing it to get a really good look. It was old – maybe hundreds of years old – and was written on some strange material that wasn't quite paper. It was something soft like a suede fabric. The writing was really weird – hard to read and old-fashioned, with lots of squiggles and strange spellings.

Puzzled, I sat closer to the lamp and started to read.

I remembered how interested Rafe had been that day in the kitchen back home when I'd mentioned the Riddle. His voice was urgent when he'd asked me where I'd heard about it – like he knew something already. I looked at the words again. I knew they were really important, but I didn't know what they meant. And if I didn't know what they meant, they wouldn't be very helpful in my search for the truth about the Ormond Singularity.

Maybe Rafe already had a copy of the text – and maybe he knew what it meant. It was possible Dad had told him something about it.

I dismissed the idea after a little thought. It would be too dangerous to try and find out. If I got caught, I'd never find the truth.

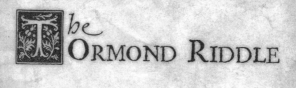

The ORMOND RIDDLE

Eight are the Leaves on my Ladyes Grace

Fayre sits the Rounde of my Ladyes Face

Thirteen Teares from the Sunnes grate Doore

Make right to treadde in Gules on the Floore

But adde One in for the Queenes fayre Sinne

Then alle shall be tolde and the Yifte unfold

I tried reading it again and again, but I couldn't make much sense of it. Something about leaves, a lady's face, tears, the sun, a grate, a door and a queen . . . Ever since I'd seen that phrase "Ormond Riddle" written on the piece of paper at Rafe's place, I had been desperate to see this. But now it had me scratching my head. I tried calling Boges again, hoping his brainpower might help, but I still couldn't get a signal.

I leaned back on the bench, frustrated and exhausted. All my efforts to get my hands on this thing had resulted in nothing but eight lines of gibberish. Great, I thought bitterly. So this was the famous Ormond Riddle that I'd been trying to find out about and that two criminal gangs were chasing. As far as I was concerned, they were welcome to the thing. And so was Rafe. I'd hoped it was going to take me closer to solving the mystery of Dad's discovery and his drawings. Instead, all I had was eight lines of nothing!

Eight? Hang on. I looked again. There were only six lines here! I remembered distinctly how the Ormond Riddle had been described on the website Boges and I had found at the library:

The Ormond Riddle—a riddle consisting of eight lines—appeared in the sixteenth century, and is thought to have originated in Tudor England.

If that description was accurate, what had happened to the last two lines? And then I noticed something that I hadn't spotted before: the last line of writing sat close to the bottom edge, whereas on the other three sides there was space. When I looked closer, I could see that the bottom edge seemed to have been neatly cut with something sharp.

Someone must have cut off the last two lines to make it harder to figure this thing out!

I turned my attention to the other documents in the folder — two letters — and began reading the first one, which was from Oriana de la Force to a legal firm.

RIANA DE LA FORCE
Legal Services

26 February

Hobson and Doddle
Lawyers

Your firm has been recommended as the leading expert in estate and inheritance law. Our client asks your opinion of the enclosed material.

As you will see, time is of the essence, especially given the law's slow pace. Our client must take action on any claim immediately as the Ormond Singularity ceases on 31 December this year.

Oriana de la Force

December 31st! All I could see was that date. It hit me like a ton of bricks. And then I remembered the desperate face of the crazy guy who'd staggered after me on New Year's Eve last year, scaring the living daylights out of me. "The Ormond Singularity!" he'd croaked. "Don't let it be the death of you too, boy! You must hide — lie low until midnight of *December 31st!*"

How had he known that? Who was he? Some sort of visionary from the future? His words echoed in my head. *They killed your father!* he'd said. Was there truth in that too? And who were "they?"

Dad got sick in Ireland, was sent home, was admitted to the hospice and then died. He'd contracted an aggressive virus that attacked his brain and killed him — quickly. It was as simple as that. I watched him deteriorate. There wasn't any "they" involved.

What was supposed to happen at midnight on December 31st? What did it mean that the Ormond Singularity would "cease to exist" on that day? Was the Singularity something to do with Dad's estate? Is that why Rafe was involved somehow? Is *that* what both the criminal gangs were after when they kept questioning me? I felt dizzy with questions.

I started reading the second letter.

Hobson&Doddle
SOLICITORS · PROCTORS · ATTORNEYS

March 13th

Dear Madam,

We write in answer to yours of the 26th of February. Should you have occasion to write to us again, pray refer to ourselves by our proper entitlement and qualification.

It is our opinion that should the Singularity be admitted to probate and the sole heir and beneficiary of the Ormond Singularity accede to the inheritance, the heir's position would survive any attack through the courts and be legally unchallengeable, and thus would be wholly secure. Unless, of course, the heir should untimely predecease the repeal of said Singularity.

That the Ormond Singularity is still active is beyond doubt, although awaiting repeal. Moreover, that several other ancient codicils, closely resembling the Ormond Singularity, have been ratified several times since their legal creation in the reign of Edward I is likewise beyond doubt.

However, our investigations show that only the Ormond Singularity may be seen as both active and relating to a living claim.

Any legal challenge, were one conceived, would be complex and of exceedingly long duration; to succeed difficult enough, to do so by December 31st impossible, in our judgment. Hence, by reason equally of the lack of an arguable case and the likely effluxion of time to pursue it, we strongly advise against such a challenge.

Should you, nevertheless, determine upon such an ill-advised course, we shall be happy to assist subject to agreement as to fees; as to which our account is presented for your kind attention.

Your obedient servant,

Ambrose Dinsdale Doddle
Partner

Oriana had clearly been asking lawyers — experts in estate and inheritance law — for advice about the Ormond Singularity. And even though the letter from "Doddle" made barely any sense to me, and I had no idea what "effluxion" meant, it was something about the short amount of time until the Ormond Singularity was repealed — became invalid. Had Dad been the heir who'd "predeceased" the repeal of the Singularity? I was confused.

I wasn't sure who Edward the First was, but I knew he'd lived a long time ago. My family name was tangled up with some really crazy things — like an angel and a riddle, and now a "singularity." But the date . . . the date had blazed off the paper. It seemed to be the most important thing.

I could hardly believe what I'd just read. It all seemed unreal.

I shoved the letters back into the folder.

Here I was, stuck in a hut in the middle of nowhere. So many people were chasing me, and I couldn't even make a phone call. Worst of all, I couldn't be near my family, or my little sister in her hospital bed. All of this seemed to have occurred because of a series of weird pictures my dad had drawn, a useless, incomplete riddle with my family's name stuck to it and a stolen item from a suitcase. And of course, the Ormond Singularity — right here in front of me I had the documents to prove that it was something very real and very dangerous — something that made people go to extreme lengths to get their hands on it. And it "ceased to exist" on *December 31st*.

My brain felt like it had been wrenched out of my head, shoved in the washing machine, then shaken out and shoved back into my skull again.

I couldn't stay still. I got up, edgy and strung out, trying to make sense of it all. After what I'd just read, the crazy guy's warning about 365 days sure didn't seem so crazy after all.

There was a deadline. And somehow he'd known about it. Who was he, and why did he care enough to warn me?

*Dead*line. I didn't like the sound of that. Like "flatline," it spelled the end of everything.

The nightmare I was living had suddenly become even deeper and darker. Could it be true that this Ormond Singularity was hundreds of years old and that it involved my family? I paced the length of the small hut before stopping in front of the ancient document — the Riddle —

that was lying on the table. What are you trying to tell me? I asked it. I stared at it, like I was actually waiting for an answer.

I stood up and checked that the door was now locked. I pulled out one of the cots, badly needing more sleep. As the first cot came free of the others, it dislodged one of the boxes on the end of the dusty shelf.

A sound from outside alerted me, and I turned the kerosene lamp down. I stood still in the darkness, straining to listen. All I could hear were the trees rustling, the calls of night birds, the chirping of crickets and the low croaking of frogs. I was getting jumpy, imagining things. But I couldn't take any chances after the close call with Sumo earlier.

An uneasy feeling started niggling at me. What if he was still out there, determined to find me?

I picked up the pepper spray and slowly opened the door, peering out into the darkness, ready to spray any intruders. I waited a few moments, then, satisfied I'd been imagining things, I closed the door again and locked it.

Curious now to see what was in the boxes, I turned up the lamp and began checking them out. I began with the one that had been dislodged.

DEPARTMENT OF DEFENSE

Item #5476
NIGHT GOGGLES

Cool! I grabbed a wrench that was lying on the ground nearby to pry it open and found inside what looked like big, freaky binoculars. These could definitely come in handy, I thought, lifting out a pair and pulling the straps over my head.

They were heavy and uncomfortable and turned the dim world I was in various shades of red. I turned my head from left to right. I could definitely see things more clearly, but it was almost like looking down a tunnel.

I reached for my backpack so I could add them to my growing armory, which now included:

tranquilizer syringes, one police-issue pepper spray, a couple of train detonators, and now, night goggles! I was going to need to find a way to keep them safe and away from prying eyes. As I stashed it all away, I couldn't help feeling like a computer game character adding to his arsenal. Except, unlike one of those two-dimensional guys, this was *real*, and I only had one life left.

In the other boxes, I found some very shriveled-looking ration packs, tin camping ovens and cooking utensils, and at the bottom of the last one, a couple of old maps.

DEPARTMENT OF DEFENSE

Item #252
VEGETABLE
RATION PACK

DEPARTMENT OF DEFENSE

Item #250
CHOCOLATE
RATION PACK

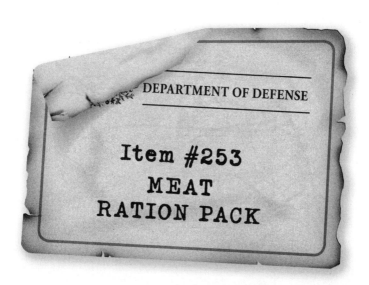

DEPARTMENT OF DEFENSE

Item #253
MEAT
RATION PACK

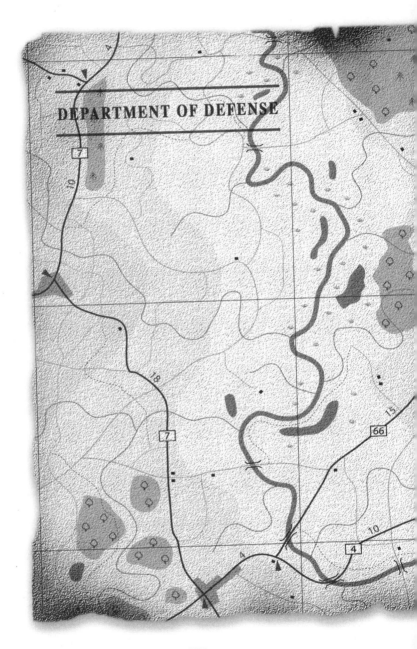

DEPARTMENT OF DEFENSE

Scale: 1:100

N

I spread the first map out on the table. I knew that while I'd come a long way, I was still pretty far from Mount Helicon and Great-uncle Bartholomew. Someone had shaded a large area around the hut and back towards the creek with pencil and had scribbled something in the nearby margin.

I put the maps in my bag and slowly glanced around the hut. Clearly this wasn't an overnight camper cabin. It was a shelter belonging to the Department of Defense, to be used by soldiers on bivouacs and exercises. From the look of the dusty equipment, it hadn't been used in a long time.

My eyes were going bleary I was so tired. I unfolded a cot, locked it into position, and let myself sink into it. A few hours' shut-eye would be perfect. I could wake up early and get away at first light. Then I'd be free to try my luck again at finding a way to Mount Helicon and Great-uncle Bartholomew. Maybe an old guy like him would be able to help with the old-fashioned language of the Ormond Riddle. Maybe he'd even know something about the Ormond Singularity and the menace that was threatening our family.

Department of Defense hut

5:03 am

I sat up, eyes wide open. It was still dark, but I knew I'd only been asleep for a couple of hours. The kerosene lamp was still on, but low, sputtering and almost out. I strained to listen in the flickering light — again on red alert.

For a change, it was the total silence that spooked me. Before, when I had gone to sleep, there'd been the night rustlings of tiny creatures, birds and the chirping of crickets. Now there was just this silence — too deep, too empty.

Something had spooked the crickets. Something had silenced the frogs. Something was out there.

I turned the kerosene lamp off completely and crept over to the door, picking up the night goggles from my bag on the way. Slowly, silently, I opened the door just a fraction and looked out. All I could see was the dim outline of a nearby tree and then nothing but the wide blackness of the scrub. Now the silence seemed full of danger.

I stepped back into the hut, slung my backpack over my shoulder, and pulled the night goggles on tight, then looked around the crack of the door at the same scene.

What I saw made me jump right back inside! I slammed the door, cold with panic!

I wrenched on my sneakers, checked that the Riddle folder and my dad's drawings were in my backpack and then slid over to the window. Keeping very close to the wall, I peered out through the night goggles at the crimson-tinted scene.

There, stealthily moving from tree to tree, no more than twenty yards away and gaining on the hut, was Sumo! But how did he know where I was? How had he tracked me, following my trail in the dark? We were in a massive area of bushland! I was miles from the scene of the accident! Was he just lucky?

Even if the low light from the lamp had been visible, I could have been anywhere! My brain was racing, trying to figure it out, but I didn't have time to deal with puzzles, and I had to get out of the hut. I couldn't possibly stay — he'd only have to smash through the window to get inside.

There was only one thing to do — act swiftly.

I kicked the door open and bolted into the night, the night goggles showing me which branches and fallen logs to avoid.

In a matter of seconds he was thundering after me, yelling and thrashing through the bush.

Branches whipped my face and scratched my arms as I charged through the scrub. I didn't have a lot of strength left, but I had to get away from this guy. I had the advantage — night goggles — while he was wildly swinging around a flashlight to light his path.

Another beam of flashlight in front of me caused me to stop dead in my tracks. I jumped back behind the shelter of a huge, hollow tree trunk. *What the . . . ?* My guts clenched.

Someone else was heading my way! My chest ached as I peered back out towards the light. It wasn't just Sumo I had to deal with — I was trapped between two of Oriana de la Force's men. Kelvin was back!

There were now two of them against me. Two thugs with flashlights.

5:19 am

Both of their flashlights suddenly switched off simultaneously; they didn't want to give away their positions. But what they didn't know was that I could see them regardless. I watched as their pinkish-red figures crept carefully towards each other. Sumo looked at Kelvin and nodded his head in my direction.

Before I knew what was going on, something

whizzed past my head. I dropped to the ground as shots rang out!

I couldn't believe it! They were shooting at me!

Another bullet whistled past me, followed a second or two later by the cracking sound of the shot. How could they see me? Were they just firing randomly, to frighten me out into the open? This was crazy!

I stayed down, hugging myself in fear. If I didn't move, they wouldn't see me. But if I didn't move, I couldn't get away. I was trapped.

Trying to make no sound, I started crawling away. I crept low along the uneven ground like a snake, for fear of raising a limb too high and catching a bullet.

Every now and then another bullet whizzed through the air near me. Somehow they still had me in their sights.

I couldn't hear *them* anywhere; I could only hear the sounds of gunfire.

Ahead, beside a huge tree, I could see a big, clumpy bush growing out of a rocky ledge. Together, the ledge and the foliage made a sort of roof. I crawled to it and huddled there, listening as bullets continued to shoot around me haphazardly.

5:28 am

I'd been huddled in the shelter of the bush for about ten minutes. The shooting had become very intermittent. Maybe they'd lost me. Or I'd lost them. I realized I could hear the sound of the highway some distance away. My frantic scrambling had brought me closer to the road.

Despite the throbbing pain of exhaustion in my legs, I decided I had to try to run for it. With the night goggles I still had some advantage over them. Once the sun rose, I would lose that. I *had* to make a break for it before sunrise.

I thought I'd climb up onto the ledge and continue from higher ground.

But when I reached up, I nearly passed out with shock and fear. Right above me, and grinning down at me, was the face of the sumo wrestler.

He reached his hands out, ready to jump off the ledge and attack me. I launched myself sideways and behind a tree trunk.

There was a loud thud as another shot filled the air between us.

I glanced up to find Sumo toppling forward, crashing a yard or so down to the ground beside me. As his round body rolled helplessly to the side, I saw a growing, dark stain on his back.

He'd been shot!

He'd been shot? What? Kelvin must have accidentally shot him!

I sprang to my feet to run, when I suddenly remembered something I'd seen on the map back at the hut: the scribbled note written in the margin that I'd casually skimmed over.

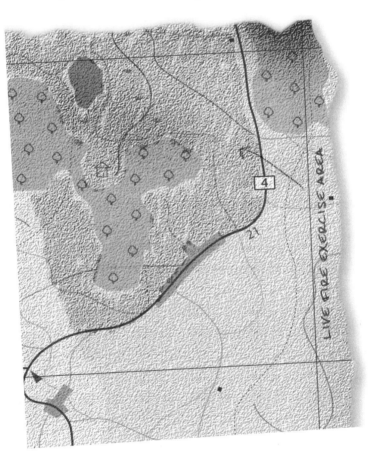

Sumo, Kelvin and I had all stumbled into the middle of an overnight Defense Force live fire exercise! Where soldiers train with live ammunition instead of blanks — firing *real* bullets!

I didn't know what to do. If I attempted to get to the road, I could meet the same fate as Sumo and get caught in the crossfire! And if I stuck around, Kelvin could be on to me in a matter of seconds.

I crawled back towards Sumo's motionless body. As I approached, thinking that I would climb up onto the high ground from where he'd just fallen and run, Sumo moved an arm and moaned. I kept an eye on him as I clambered up onto the rock ledge, ignoring as much as I could the pain in my legs and the hot ache in my inflamed shoulder. If I could figure out where the firing was coming from using the night goggles, I might have a chance of avoiding it by going around the soldiers and making it to the road.

Very carefully, using a nearby tree trunk as protection, I scanned around three hundred and sixty degrees, panning through the trees and bushes. I saw a group of soldiers some distance away, lying on their stomachs, their weapons directed straight at me!

Did they know we were there? I couldn't quite make out their faces, so I didn't know if they were wearing night goggles or not.

I dropped flat to the ground while all around me bullets whizzed once more! Fragments of shattered timber from the trees splintered and struck me, piercing my bare hands with stinging strength. I curled up into a tiny ball.

Finally the firing stopped. The shrieking of the bullets was gone, and I realized just how loudly I was panting.

The soldiers looked like they were dug in, so I figured I was the one who needed to move. I set off crawling backwards, through spiky, prickly scrub, moving in a wide arc, hoping to end up behind them.

It was taking a long time to get anywhere, and I was still worrying about Kelvin being out there somewhere.

6:12 am

I'd almost made it. I could see the occasional car on the road with its headlights still bright despite dawn streaking the eastern sky. A little bit farther, and I'd be at the road. I eased my heavy backpack off and took out my cell phone.

At last I had a signal, but not for long. My

battery was almost dead. I badly needed to charge my phone so that I could call Boges and so that he could call me. I shoved my phone back in my bag, shouldered the heavy thing again and started walking parallel to the highway on the lookout for a gas station. I hoped that by now Kelvin was a long way away and not cruising the highway, looking for me. Or worse, creeping up on me from behind.

An ambulance flew by in a blur behind the trees ahead, and I guessed that the army had found their accidental victim, Sumo. I couldn't help smiling. That was one less thug I had to worry about — at least for a while.

7:29 am

The sun was well and truly up now, and it was hot walking as I threaded my way towards the road. Through the gaps I caught a glimpse of the big signage of a gas station in the distance, where I knew I could get a drink of water and maybe something to eat.

Ridgetop Service Station

8:17 am

Warily, I checked out the place from my position

across the road, wondering whether the cops had issued a warning about me being on the loose in the area. I couldn't see any of the vehicles I'd come to fear — the dark blue Mercedes, the black Subaru, or any kind of cop car. As I approached, I saw that there was a dining area to the left of the pumps. It was a big barn of a place, with white garden chairs and round tables and an open kitchen in the back.

The place was pretty empty, except for a couple of truckies who were gulping down big mugs of coffee and hunched over plates topped with sausages, bacon and eggs. My mouth was watering. I hoped the woman behind the counter had a heart. She reminded me of Rafe's dead wife — my Aunt Klara — with shiny brown hair in a bob and big eyes.

I checked my reflection in the window near the door and quickly smoothed my messy hair and brushed down my clothes. My face had a few scratches, but it wasn't too bad. As long as no one recognized me as the State's Most Wanted Juvenile, I was happy. I didn't think they would. I hardly even recognized myself.

8:31 am
___

I was too tired to try anything sneaky, so after

easing my backpack off and dumping it on a chair I went straight up to the counter and put all my change down.

"Excuse me," I said. "If I give you a few dollars, would you please let me use one of your outlets for a little while? I really need to charge my phone."

I pulled out my phone to show her. She looked at me curiously for a moment and then scooped the money up. "Is that all you have?" she asked.

I still had money hidden in my shoe — money I owed to Repro for helping me out back at Oriana's — but I wasn't about to bring that out.

I nodded.

She stared at me again, like she was trying to figure me out, trying to figure out what I was doing there in the middle of nowhere on my own, with a dead phone battery. "Where are you headed?" she asked.

"To my brother's place, just another hour or so up the highway," I lied, being careful not to mention Mount Helicon or my great-uncle again. "I'm hoping to get some . . . work with him," I said. "I need to make a couple of phone calls though, so it would be great I could just charge my phone for half an hour or so . . ."

"You know there's a pay phone just out there, near the big cooler," she said.

"Thanks, but I'm also expecting a couple of calls, so I really need this," I said, holding up my phone again, "charged."

She dropped the money back on the counter, then pushed it to me. "There's an outlet just over there, on the wall near the heater."

I hesitated. She was actually going to let me do it. And she'd given me my money back.

"Go on," she added. "And I'll buy you a milkshake too."

I felt all mixed up. "Thanks so much," I said. I'd been running and hiding for so long that I'd forgotten that some people could be kind, just because they wanted to be.

8:51 am

The milkshake tasted like heaven and took my mind off my hunger for a bit. I decided not to use up the last of my change on food. There was nothing on the menu that I could afford with that amount anyway — but I could get some bread, or a bag of potatoes . . . and if I could find some way of cooking them . . . The thought of Mum's awesome mashed potatoes made my stomach churn. I felt a sudden rush of grief and pain when I thought of my mum and my lost home and tried to think of something else instead.

9:01 am

While my phone was charging, I went to call Boges, but was stopped by a flood of voicemail messages and text messages from him. I ignored them because I wanted to talk to him right away. I was dying to tell him how we'd gotten hold of the Riddle.

I dialed his number and waited, scraping the foam from the sides of the milkshake glass with my straw. I felt almost safe here in this sunny dining area, with the kitchen staff bustling from the doorway behind the counter and the kind woman nearby taking someone else's order. Kelvin was a long way away, I hoped.

I couldn't get through to Boges immediately, so I thought I'd wait for a moment and call again. Meanwhile, I spread out the other map I'd taken from the army hut. This showed that Ridgetop, where I was sitting now, was located somewhere between the coast where I'd come from and the mountain range further west where my great-uncle lived.

Our home suburb of Richmond was marked, back towards the city. I thought about Mum. And

Gabbi. I hoped she was getting better. She was young and strong. Surely she'd pull through and be herself again soon, I told myself.

I pulled the Riddle out hoping that this morning, after the sugar-hit of the milkshake, my brain would have been boosted. Slowly, I read it through again.

My brain-boosting theory didn't hold up. The Ormond Riddle was a total non-starter.

I redialed Boges's number. If anyone was going to get what it meant, it would be him.

"Boges!" I said, so glad to hear him pick up.

"Dude! Where have you been? I've been calling and calling! I left heaps of messages for you. You OK?"

"I've been completely out of range and then completely out of battery," I said. "Now listen up! I found some really, really important stuff at Oriana de la Force's place. Repro helped me bust in and search her study. And guess what I've found? You won't believe what I've got right here in my hands!"

I had the strong feeling that Boges wasn't paying a great deal of attention to what I was saying.

"Something's happened," he said.

"You bet something's happened! I've got it

right here, in front of me!" I was just about to mention the Riddle when I realized Boges wasn't listening at all.

"Cal," he said seriously, "you've gotta come back home."

"Tell me what's going on," I demanded quickly, feeling sick with anxiety.

Boges paused. I could hear him sigh before saying, "They're talking about switching the Gabster's life support off."

"What?" I couldn't believe what he'd just said. It wasn't possible. "What are you talking about? Why? Why would they do that? It's only been, like, not even three months!"

"I'm so sorry, but you heard me right. Apparently if she doesn't respond soon, they're going to switch the machine off."

"But they can't do that!" I said. "Mum would never let them! It's not right!"

Boges sighed deeply again. "I've been desperate to contact you!" he continued, now more urgent and commanding. "You've gotta do something to stop them! I've been trying to let you know, to tell you to come back! Things have changed a lot in the last twenty-four hours. They did some major scan of her brain, and it looks like she's got this damage that means —

well — it means that she's never gonna be right and that she could be in pain. It's bad, dude. Unless a miracle happens — or someone stops them — they're turning her life support off. Your mum says she doesn't want her to suffer any more . . ."

I tried to speak, but my voice wouldn't work.

"Whether it's right or wrong, you've gotta come back if you want to see your little sister alive again," Boges urged me. "If Gabbi could hear your voice it just might make all the difference. I bet she senses that you're not around. If you talked to her, you might be able to help her wake up and come out of it. Your voice might just be the miracle. You've gotta go and see her! You're the closest person in the world to her. If you do that and there's some improvement in her condition, they'll stop talking like this! Come back now! The Gabster's running out of time!" Boges's voice cracked. I could hear that he was almost crying. "I wish I could do something, Cal, but you're the only one that can save her."

For a few seconds shock made me blind. I blinked to clear my head. I felt dizzy, and when I looked around the dining area it seemed to be swirling. If Gabbi's life support was turned off, she would die. *My sister would die.* I would *never* see her again. I felt my entire strength spill out of me like water. Solving the Ormond Riddle right now meant nothing.

"When?"

"I don't know exactly when, but your mum said she wants to give her one more week."

"I'm coming home," I said. Then I remembered I didn't have a home. "I'll come straight to the hospital. I'll hitchhike, I'll steal a car, or I'll walk if I have to. I'll be there!"

I hung up and ripped my charger out of the outlet. My heart was racing. I shoved everything into my bag, threw it over my shoulder and looked out at the speeding traffic on the road outside. I ran out the door without a sideways glance. Change of plans again. I had to get to the hospital. I had to get to the city. ASAP.

9:49 am

I'd wandered around the side of the gas station to the pay phone that the lady at the diner had mentioned earlier. I had to call Mum. I was such a long way from her and Gabbi, and I needed to see if I could talk some sense into her.

My heart nearly fell out when I heard her voice. There were so many things I wanted to say — to tell her, to ask her, but this wasn't the time.

"Mum, it's me. I've just heard the news about Gabbi — that you're talking about switching off the life support! You can't! You mustn't!"

"Cal! Darling! Is it really you? Are you all right? Where have you been? Why haven't you called me? Would you please just come home to me? I've been out of my mind — and now with Gabbi the way she is . . ."

"You can't do this!" I cried. "You can't switch off her life support system! You've got to stop it! Are you crazy? You've got to let her live!"

"Cal, you're not here! You don't understand the situation! You don't know what it's like seeing her day after day like this — so thin and wasted. The doctors say she could be suffering and not able to let us know. I just can't let it go on . . ." Her voice trailed off, taken over by sobbing. "I'd be selfish to want to keep her alive in this state . . ." she added. "I keep talking it over with Rafe. He doesn't know what to do either, but he's leaving the decision to me. If she's suffering, Cal, then I don't think we have a choice. I can't bear to think of her being in pain, and not being able to tell us!"

My mother's voice broke once more, and she sobbed loudly into the phone. I thought about what she'd said. I knew it would be terrible to be helpless and in pain, but unable to tell anyone.

"Can't they just try giving her painkillers?"

"It's not as simple as that, Cal. Drugs could *kill* someone in her condition."

"But you're going to *kill* her anyway, so what does it matter!"

"How can you say that to *me*!?" Mum screamed. "*You're* the reason for all of this! *You* put her in that hospital bed! And now you're just running around like a madman! Give yourself up already!"

Her words ripped my heart out.

"I'm sorry," she pleaded, seconds later, through hopeless tears. "I'm just so upset, Cal. I didn't mean to say that to you. It's all too much. I know it's not your fault you're the way you are!"

"Mum," I said, using all my strength to ignore what she had said. I couldn't waste my time getting upset by what she thought of me. "I'm coming back. I'll be there as soon as I can. Just promise me you won't let them do it — not until I get there. I *have* to see her. I'm her big brother. Promise me?"

A dark blue car pulled up alongside a pump. It wasn't the Mercedes I'd come to know so well;

it was a big six-cylinder job with a lowered body and fat wheels, and the driver wasn't looking for gas. Right away I knew what it was.

An unmarked police car.

They were on to me. When I saw the driver getting out of it, I panicked, looking around for somewhere else to run. I had a tall fence behind me that was way too high for me to get over.

"Just promise me you won't do anything until I get there!" I shouted to my sobbing mother, before hanging up. I slipped out of the booth and headed for a door that looked like it led to the bathrooms.

I flung the door open, and as it swung closed behind me, I dashed into the men's room.

It was empty. I raced into one of the stalls which had a window high up on the wall. If I climbed on top of the cistern and heaved myself up, I might be able to get out to the rear of the building and back to the cover of the bushland.

I closed the door and was about to climb up when I heard someone enter the bathroom. Someone with heavy footsteps. Was it the cop?

It was. I could see his bulky, state-issued, general-purpose boots over near the sinks. His portable radio chattered away. Was every police car in the area looking for me?

"Copy, base," he said.

I heard the sound of running water in the sink. He must have just been freshening up, washing his hands.

He continued talking into his portable radio. "I'll wait here and then we'll coordinate the search when the other cars arrive. We might have to widen the perimeters."

I remained frozen, hunched up on the closed toilet seat. I was petrified, just wanting to get out of there! Get on the road, get to the city, and get to my little sister. Instead, I was stuck in a rural bathroom.

It seemed an eternity before the cop turned off the water, dried his hands and finally walked back out.

10:20 am

The window was fixed, so I had no option but to break it. I waited until I heard a huge and noisy rig going through gear changes as it slowed and parked near a pump. Using the noise as a cover, I wrapped my hoodie around my fist and punched hard into the glass. The first blow broke through, but then I had to waste more time knocking out the jagged edges of glass that remained stuck in the wooden frame.

Standing on top of the cistern, I shoved my backpack out through the broken window and then heaved myself up to follow it. Once I got my head and shoulders through, I saw that I was looking down onto the back of the service station as I'd hoped, and there was no one around. I hauled myself all the way through the window frame, then dropped heavily to the ground several yards below, rolling with the fall.

I grabbed my backpack and took off past the dumpsters and a stack of large oil drums, into the bush once more.

I had to stay under cover and follow the road. For all I knew there could be roadblocks set up, and even if I hitched a ride, there was always the danger that we'd be pulled over and my identity would be discovered. Even though I was gutted from my conversation with my mum, and I could hardly see straight, the thought of Gabbi lying in such danger spurred me on.

11:51 am

I'd jogged several miles — stumbling through the scrub not far from the road — before reassuring myself that there were no roadblocks leading away from the service station. The cop in the bathroom had talked about waiting for the others to get there and widening the perimeters of the search. That could take time to put in place. But for now it looked OK.

I thought of Gabbi again. My exhausted body ached, and I knew I wasn't thinking quite clearly. But I had to take the risk.

I stuck my right thumb out into the traffic as I hurried along the road, signaling that I wanted a ride. My legs were trembling, but I forced myself onwards. I had to get to the city. I had to get to the hospital. I knew it was dangerous to hitchhike, but what else could I do?

I'm coming, Gabs, I kept saying under my breath. *I'm coming*. Those words somehow kept me going. I broke into a run.

I was so shocked when a car finally pulled up for me that I'd opened the passenger door and was halfway in the car before I saw who was driving it!

I was out of there like a flash, leaving the door swinging, running like anything away from him! His door slammed shut, and I knew he was coming after me.

I had to ditch the backpack — it was so heavy, and if he caught me he would have the drawings! I had no time to do anything like dig around and find the pepper spray or a detonator — but the weight of it was slowing me down. As I ran, I kept scanning for a safe place to hide it — throw it if necessary.

He was gaining on me. He'd hesitated once before, back in Oriana de la Force's study, giving me the chance to escape through the window, but he wasn't giving me any chances now — Kelvin was set on capturing me!

Fear gave me a lot of speed, and I climbed over a high fence that blocked the way. It was a serious fence, with triple strands of barbed wire running along it. To get over, I had to use my jacket wrapped around my hands, but I still snagged my jeans, tearing them as I dropped to my feet on the other side.

Just ahead of me was a large tree with spreading branches and thick foliage. Best of all, there was a hollow at shoulder height, so I swiftly pulled my backpack off and tossed it into the cavity. I heard Kelvin shouting behind me and glanced back. He hadn't seen anything — he was snagged on the fence, struggling and making it worse. For once, I'd been given a lucky break — spared some time — so I retrieved my bag and continued running with it back over my shoulder.

I raced past the tree and split sideways,

running across a field. Not slowing my pace, I chanced to look backwards to see where Kelvin was. His small, far-away figure was still stuck on the fence, flailing and shouting. I kept going.

There had to be a way for me to get back to the city — back to my little sister. Back to save her life. I headed towards a little house I'd noticed, nestled under flowering trees. I was hoping that out here, people mightn't have heard of the crazy kid the whole state was looking for.

Black smoke rose from the chimney like a smoke signal.

12:32 pm

I edged closer. A small car was parked outside, and as I watched, hidden behind a tree, I saw two elderly ladies, one carrying an overnight bag, heading towards the car. I could hear their conversation quite easily.

"It's been so lovely visiting, Rhonda, but I must get back to Timmy. And it'll take me at least a couple of hours or so to get back to Valley Heights."

Rhonda stood near the car while her friend opened the trunk and put the overnight bag in. "I keep thinking I've left something behind," she added, standing beside the open trunk.

Valley Heights was a couple of hours closer to the city. But I gave myself a reality check. I couldn't imagine a sweet old lady giving a lift to a street kid like me. She'd probably have a heart attack at the sight of me.

"Goodness me," she said, shaking her head. "Now I remember. My new lipstick. I've left it in your bathroom."

The two of them went back inside, and I saw my chance. I hurried over to the trunk and checked it out. Apart from a large, red tartan travel blanket and the small overnight bag, the spacious trunk was empty. I climbed in and huddled down, pulling the blanket over me. I hoped she wouldn't look too closely in here, and I'd be able to figure out how to open it from the inside. I also hoped "Timmy" wasn't going to turn out to be her son — someone who might easily take me down if he found out I'd hidden in his elderly mother's trunk.

I could hear their voices returning, and within a few moments the trunk slammed shut, leaving me in darkness. I never thought I'd be curled in the back of a trunk by choice, not after being thrown in one against my will by Oriana's thugs the first time they grabbed me.

The ignition started, and I heard Rhonda's

voice calling, "Have a safe trip, Melba, dear!" as the car slowly crunched over the gravel and into the street. A short while later I could hear the sounds of the highway. Melba's car paused, no doubt waiting for a break in the traffic, before turning onto the highway on the way to Valley Heights.

12:51 pm

I was pretty uncomfortable, but relieved that I was finally on my way back to the city and to the hospital, to stop them turning off Gabbi's life support.

Even if there was a roadblock, I couldn't imagine the police suspecting Melba of aiding and abetting the most wanted fugitive in the state. At least that's what I told myself.

We cruised along, and I tried to catch some sleep, but it was impossible. Images of Gabbi kept haunting me — looking like she did that day in January when I'd found her, pale and unconscious, barely breathing, in a heap on the floor of my old house.

3:40 pm

The car had stopped, and I heard the front door slam. Somewhere, close by, a dog was barking.

"Now, now, Timmy," I heard Melba shout out, her voice getting clearer as she came around to the trunk. "Mama's back home again. Just let me get unpacked first, and then we can catch up."

Timmy was just a dog! I heard a click as the trunk was released. Soft light fell through the weave of the red tartan blanket that was covering me, and cool air gushed around me. I felt movement nearby as Melba picked up her overnight bag.

"You can come out now," she said.

I was too stunned to move for a moment. Was she talking to me?

"Young man, you can come out now," she repeated.

The old girl had known I was in there all along!

Sheepishly, I pulled the blanket off me. "I'm sorry," I said, "I just really needed a lift . . . I hope I haven't scared you."

I climbed out of the trunk, lugging my backpack out with me. Nearby, a dog was going bananas.

"A stowaway, eh? I must say, I've never had one before, but don't worry, I'm not afraid in the slightest. I've seen a whole lot in my life more frightening than a boy in a trunk. Especially not a scruffy, skinny one like you. You look like you could do with a good hot meal . . . and a bath."

A hot meal? Was she nuts?

She gestured to her bag, as if she was telling me to carry it for her, so I quickly picked it up and followed her as she walked up the front garden path and onto the shady porch of her cottage house.

"Settle down, Timmy. We've got a visitor for the night," she said to the dog. It was jumping at the front door, scratching and whimpering.

"Thanks," I said, thinking how much I'd love a home-cooked meal and somewhere to sit down, "but I need to get back to the city, pretty urgently. That's the only reason I snuck into your trunk. It's really important that I get to the hospital. A family member of mine is really sick."

"That's terrible," she said, unlocking the front door. "Of course you must get there. I'd drive you myself, but I'm afraid I have other responsibilities."

The second the door opened, a small, white, yappy little dog with a rhinestone collar launched itself at me, snarling and snapping.

"Don't mind Timmy, he's just excited that we have a guest with us. Please come in," she said, stepping back to let me inside. "My name's Mrs. Melba Snipe."

The crazy little dog was leaping up at my knees, biting my jeans.

"Tom," I said, extending my hand to her, avoiding the leaping mutt who seemed to want to take my fingers off. I was still in shock from her reaction to me, but I took her hand and shook it. It was so small and frail — her skin moved like tissue paper.

We walked down the hallway and into her living room while the yappy dog still jumped around us. Mrs. Snipe unlocked a sliding door that opened out to a grassy backyard. She gave the dog a little push outside, poured him some dog food into a bowl sitting on a mat out there, and then slid the door shut again.

I put her bag down and took a look around the living room. The carpet was thick, and an unusual shade of green. The walls too, were green and had a floral wallpaper border running along their middles. Everywhere I looked, surfaces were covered with flowers — plastic, silk, paper. They stood in vases, in jars, on dishes and plates. They stuck out of bottles and brackets on the wall. Even the window sills were swamped with them.

The walls in the kitchen were different — they were covered in heaps of tightly packed frames holding old photographs of people, mostly black-and-white pictures of two particular men: one in uniform and another one who could have been his brother, or son.

"I must get back to the city, Mrs. Snipe," I said. "It's a matter of life and death."

Something cooking in the nearby kitchen made me realize again how hungry I was. I followed Melba over to it.

"Before I left yesterday to visit Rhonda," she said, as she slipped a delicate hand into a polka dot oven mitt and then lifted the heavy lid of a pot, "I put a casserole on in my slow cooker. It should be done to a T by now. You must stay and have something to eat. You're looking a little pale."

She stirred the simmering pot. I had never smelled anything better in my life, but I felt restless, I couldn't keep still.

She turned back to me from the stove. "Here, pull up a chair."

I was edgy with anxiety, but I sat down anyway. I needed to eat. I watched as Melba filled a kettle with water from the faucet, and then carried it carefully over to the stove.

Before long it was whistling.

"Tea?" she asked, adding a couple of bags to the pot.

"Sure, thanks."

She bent down to a little cupboard and pulled out two completely mismatched sets of fine teacups and saucers, a small creamer and a sugar bowl. They, like the rest of the place, were floral and had wide mouths and ornate handles.

"Fetch me those two bowls over there, will you, pet?"

I followed her eyes to a pair of white bowls and picked them up. When I turned back to the table, my teacup was filled to the brim and steaming. Melba leaned over with the slow cooker pot and a ladle and dished us both out a good helping of her casserole.

It was delicious. I wolfed it down so fast it was like I'd forgotten I had teeth for chewing. When Melba offered a second helping, I happily accepted. In return, she seemed pleased to have company and someone to feed.

"Mrs. Snipe, that was *so* good," I said, after practically licking my bowl clean. "That was one big casserole."

"Yes, I always cook for two, at least," she responded, promptly.

"For two?"

"Well, in spite of my age, I'm not crazy," she said with a giggle. "I know it's only me here . . . but old habits die hard." The dog barked sharply from outside, like he was interrupting her. "Oh, and you, Timmy," she added, raising her voice in the direction of the bark from outside. "How could I forget you?"

"I'm glad I could help you eat it," I said.

"Me too, dear. It's been a long time since Mr. Snipe left us," she said sadly, "but not a day goes by without me thinking of him. We met when we were just sixteen, you know."

Wow, I thought. I was fifteen, almost sixteen. It was hard to imagine this frail, old woman in front of me ever being my age.

"Is that him?" I asked, gesturing to the many photos of the man in uniform hanging neatly on the wall by the fridge.

She smiled and nodded. "Yes, that's him. The lovely chap in the photo next to him is my son," she said. "Shall I put another pot on, then?"

6:02 pm

Over another cup of tea, Mrs. Snipe seemed to want to know all about my sick family member, and I ended up pretty much telling her the truth. Well, the truth without all the gory details, like revealing the fact that I was a fugitive and why. When she asked me how my little sister had come to be on life support, I mumbled something vague about a bad fall she'd had while bushwalking. I also told the story that I'd been working up and down the coast, helping with deliveries.

"I'm pooped. I know it's only early, but I think I'm going to have to head off to bed," Melba announced, when we'd both finished our tea. *Bed.* I started yawning at the thought of it.

"You're welcome to wash up and stay here for the night," she added, as she slowly lifted herself out of her seat. "No good you heading off now. And my couch is rather comfy. There are blankets and towels in the closet next to the bathroom. I suggest you have a hot shower, a good rest and then, if you must, move on early in the morning."

The sickening thoughts of Gabbi wouldn't leave my mind, but she was right. I figured I'd have a better chance of finding a way to the city in the daytime, and I was exhausted. I hadn't slept more than a few hours in the last couple of days, plus I had no idea when I'd have an opportunity like this again.

"I hope I'm not about to offend you, but your clothes are a real mess," Melba said tentatively. "Can I offer you a pair of my son's old jeans and a clean shirt? You're about the same size as he was when he was your age, years ago of course. I've actually got a box full of his things that I was going to give away. To a good cause. But I think you're probably a good enough cause."

"That'd be great." I wasn't at all offended. In fact, I was really grateful.

She led me to her son's clothes and the bathroom, before saying goodnight and disappearing into a room down at the far end of the hallway.

2 APRIL

274 days to go . . .

8:06 am

"Well look at you! That's much better, isn't it?" Melba said with satisfaction, as I stepped into the kitchen wearing my new clothes. She looked me up and down a few times and smiled warmly, then she shook her head, like she was shaking away an unwanted thought. "Toast?"

"Love some!"

I'd slept like a baby. She was right about the comfy couch. I'd woken up feeling refreshed and strong and ready to tackle whatever it was going to take to get me to Gabbi.

"Perhaps you could do a little something for me when you get to the city? A small favor," asked Melba.

"I'd be happy to," I said, smothering my toast

with a thick dollop of crunchy peanut butter. "What is it?"

Melba disappeared from the kitchen for a moment and returned with a book in a paper bag. "My friend Elvira left this here when she last visited. Would you mind popping it in her mailbox? The address is written on the back there. I'd be most grateful."

"I'll make sure your friend gets it back." I took the book and tucked it away safely in my already-bulging backpack.

"Thank you, Tom. I really feel I can rely on you." Then she frowned. "There's something awfully familiar about you."

"I've been here and there, helping with the deliveries," I said vaguely. "It's quite possible you've seen me around before."

"Perhaps it's just that you remind me so much of my son . . . Especially when you're in his clothes!"

"Ha ha," I laughed, looking down at myself. "You've been so kind, Mrs. Snipe. Especially for not saying anything about me being in the trunk. Anyone else would have flipped out!"

Melba chuckled. "Well, it certainly isn't something you see every day, but I knew you couldn't do me any harm while you were stuck in my trunk, and then when you got out, looking so miserable and hungry, I didn't have the heart to get cranky with you and send you away."

"Thanks," I said, feeling grateful.

"Now that doesn't mean you should continue with that form of transportation," Melba added, with a wave of her finger. "Not all old ladies are as fearless, or as trusting, as I am!"

"Don't worry, I'll make sure I catch the bus in the future. Thanks again for everything," I said, as I put our plates in the sink. "The first thing I'll do once I've seen my sister is deliver your friend's book to her."

"Come again, won't you?" she asked softly, with a hand on my shoulder.

"Of course."

I grabbed my things and walked down the hallway to the front door. "Say goodbye to Timmy for me," I said.

The strange little dog must have heard his name. He started yapping like crazy and running around the side of the house, probably to try and take a bite out of me in the front yard. But I was quicker. I raced down the front path and tackled the gate in a one-handed leap.

10:21 am

Cautiously, I headed back to the highway, constantly looking to my left and right. It was just as well I was alert because when I reached the turnoff, I spotted a roadblock.

A line of policemen was stopping traffic heading towards the city, and carefully checking the back seats and trunks of every vehicle. If we hadn't taken the Valley Heights exit yesterday and instead come this far, I would have given one of those officers quite a shock from my position in Melba's trunk and undoubtedly spent the night in a concrete cell.

Thanks to her kindness, food and couch, this new obstacle didn't faze me. Yeah, it meant that it would take me a lot longer to get where I was going, but I was free, and I was well and truly on my way to the hospital. That was all that mattered.

Right away I began backtracking through the bush, and when I finally felt I was close enough to the highway to keep following it, but far enough away from it not to attract any police attention, I restarted my journey.

I was running as much as I could, only slowing to walk when I felt myself really tiring, or when my backpack was feeling too heavy. I wasn't only running for my life, I was running for Gabbi's.

5:15 pm

I'd covered a lot of ground over the day and had snuck onto a property to have a quick drink from a hose. I quickly ran back over the fence and under the cover of the bush when a whoomp, whoomp, whoomp, suddenly took my attention to the sky. A helicopter had begun circling the area I was in.

The trees had started to thin out substantially, so it was becoming more and more difficult to stay out of sight. Eventually I decided to sit tight under some bushes until the sun went down.

6:22 pm

📱 boges, what's happening? any news? any changes?

📱 nothing, no & no. still have till the end of the week. where r u? everything ok?

📱 i'm cool. making my way back as fast as i can. might have 2 camp here 4 nite tho.

8:37 pm

My night goggles had come in handy again, helping me walk a few more miles in the dark. I'd put a lot of distance between me and Melba Snipe's little cottage in Valley Heights and was slowly closing the gap between me and Gab.

She had less than a week to live unless I got there in time to stop them. I didn't even care any more if I got arrested — as long as Gabbi's life support stayed on, she had a chance of recovering. Stuff the Riddle, the Angel and the

Singularity. Stuff Oriana de la Force, Vulkan Sligo . . . and Winter Frey. Stuff what Mum thought of me. Stuff it all. Right now Dad would only want me to focus on keeping his little girl alive.

9:20 pm

I found a good campsite — some soft soil sheltered by a wide tree — then pulled out almost all of my clothes so that I could layer myself in them and keep warm. Within seconds I'd curled up in my sleeping bag, one arm outstretched around my backpack, and fallen asleep.

11:01 pm

Sometime later, something woke me. I sat up in alarm and scanned the darkness. I grabbed the night goggles and held them over my eyes, looking around slowly for movement. Nothing. No one. You're just jumpy, I told myself.

Soon I'd fallen asleep again, but couldn't settle. I was drifting in and out of dreams — snippets of my recurring nightmare flashed into my consciousness, and the freezing desolation of its atmosphere chilled me into waking. The cold night air gave me no relief from the terrible vibe that the images of the white toy dog had left me with.

I sat up for a moment, huddled in my jacket, holding the guardian angel pin that Repro had given me. I rubbed my thumb over the fine details of the tiny angel's robes and wings. I sure needed an angel to look out for me. Not like the Ormond Angel, who so far had brought me nothing but trouble.

3 APRIL

273 days to go . . .

5:42 am

I sprang awake. Someone was trying to pull my backpack from me!

For a second I was dazed and confused, until I saw a stooping figure lugging my bag away.

"Give that back!" I yelled, jumping to my feet and rubbing my eyes to try and wake myself up. "What do you think you're doing? That's mine!"

Last night I'd told myself that nothing mattered, except reaching Gabbi. But I needed my bag to get me there! Shock and fear startled me. Immediately I thought of Sumo and Kelvin, tracking me down after all, but this guy . . . this guy wasn't either of them . . .

I launched at him and grabbed the backpack hard, tearing it away from him. He stumbled backwards, and I took advantage of that to throw myself on top of him. My knees held him down by his chest, and my fear turned into anger — then rage. My blood surged through me in a fury! I'd had enough of people pushing me around, threatening me, chasing me, locking me up, running me off the road, terrorizing me — and now someone was trying to steal the bag containing the only things I owned!

Furious, I started pummeling the squirming thief.

"No!" he yelled. "Please stop! Don't hit me! I'm sorry! I didn't mean to upset you! Please, I was just going to borrow it!"

I stopped. The voice that was crying out sounded like it belonged to someone my own age. I held his shoulders down.

"You're a liar!" I yelled, as we scuffled in the dirt. It wasn't hard to overpower him, and after a few moments he stopped squirming and just lay there, panting. I hadn't realized that over the past few months of living in the derelict St. Johns Street house, the storm water drain, and anywhere else I could stretch my exhausted body out, I'd toughened up a lot. I pinned his arms to the ground, squashing him again with the weight of my body.

"Please," he puffed, "let me go."

I held his wrists together with my right hand while I fished out my flashlight from the nearby backpack and shone it directly on his face.

Under the flashlight was a pale, freckle-faced, scared-looking guy who was probably about fifteen, like me. He had gelled hair sticking out in all directions, and ginger-colored eyes which were blinking and squinting.

"Who are you, and what do you want with me?" I demanded, keeping the light on his face.

"Griff — Griff Kirby," he gasped. "Nothing, I don't want nothing. Honest. I didn't mean anything bad. I just saw this backpack lying on the ground . . . and . . ."

"And me right next to it," I said. "You were going to pinch it, weren't you?"

Griff wrinkled his face.

"Kind of," he admitted.

"You're a thief! Why should I let you up? Give me one good reason!"

"Let me up, and I'll give you heaps of good reasons. A guy like me— "

"Who pinches people's backpacks while they're sleeping," I finished.

I was tired of playing games. "OK, get up. Just go," I said, releasing him from my grip. I stood up and then backed away a yard or so.

The flashlight lay on its side, dimly lighting the scene and making deep shadows. Griff Kirby slowly stood up and brushed dirt off his jeans.

"You hit pretty hard," he said, admiringly. He turned, and I thought that would be the last I'd see of him, but all he did was take a few steps towards a shoulder bag that lay on the ground near a low rock. He leaned over and pulled some things out of it. I saw a bag of chips and my mouth watered.

Food.

"You hungry?" he asked.

I ignored him, wondering what he was up to now.

"What's your name?" he asked me.

"Tom."

"Catch!" he said, as he threw the bag of chips to me.

I caught them, tore them open, and started shoving handfuls into my mouth. Griff sat down on the rock by his own bag and stared at me.

"What do you want?" I asked him, wanting to know why he was sticking around.

"Umm, nothing."

"OK . . . well I've gotta get to the city," I said, as I started packing up my things that were scattered across the ground after our struggle.

"Me too," said Griff. "We could go together. It's safer that way."

"Safer?"

"Yes," he replied. "So what's happened to you? When I see a guy in the middle of the bush, sleeping on the ground," he scoffed, "I know there's gotta be a story. Were you kicked out of home too?"

"Sort of," I said. I upended the chip bag to get the last of the crumbs and thought about what he was saying about traveling together. It made sense. Hitchhiking is dodgy at the best of times. And there was that little issue of the state looking for me — a *solo* item. Two fifteen-year-olds traveling together would be great cover for me. I was decided.

"Let's try and get a ride," I said.

Even in the dark I could see Griff's eyes light up. He slung his shoulder bag into position, and we started walking.

Roadside Gas 2 Go

9:52 am

From higher ground and well-hidden by trees and bush, Griff Kirby and I were checking out a small truck parked on the side of the road, its bed covered in some sort of canvas. The driver had gone in to pay for his fuel.

"He's pointing in the right direction," said Griff. "Let's go!"

The morning sun was rising high into the sky as we skidded down the slope as fast as we could, keeping out of sight of the store area. We crept around the back of the covered truck and squeezed our bags into it before climbing under the canvas flaps ourselves. I thought I heard the sound of another helicopter overhead as I pulled the canvas tight over us.

We waited in silence, holding our breath as the sound of the driver's footsteps approached the truck. He unlocked his door, climbed in and started the ignition.

I exhaled with relief as the vehicle picked up speed, heading towards the city. The signpost said ninety-five miles, so the trip should only take us a couple of hours, I thought.

I'm on my way, Gabbi. Just hold on for me.

We settled down in the back, making ourselves as comfortable as we could. Luckily for us, the driver had the radio up quite loud.

"See, Mum's got this new boyfriend," Griff was saying, "and he doesn't like me at all."

Instantly I thought of Mum living at Rafe's

place. Even though I knew Rafe was trying to do his best, the move to his place seemed to be taking my family further and further away from me and our old life.

"So they kicked me out," Griff shrugged. "What about you?"

"Yeah," I said, "same." I didn't want to say too much. Griff could turn into a problem for me if he knew who I was.

"You don't say much," he observed.

"It takes me a while," I said, "to buddy up with someone who was trying to rob me only this morning."

Griff gave me a friendly shove. "Sorry, dude," he said, sounding like Boges. "Being out on the street makes you do things you wouldn't normally do," he explained.

I knew about that all too well.

"But anyway," he continued, "we've got the same story — we've both been chucked out of the house — so we should stick together. That way we can look out for each other."

"I'll be looking out for my backpack," I said, "that's for sure."

Griff stifled a laugh. I wasn't sure if I needed a buddy like him.

10:30 am

"Cool ring. Where'd you get it?" Griff asked, noticing the Celtic ring on my little finger that Gabbi had given me. Maybe he had his eye on it.

"My little sister gave it to me. It was hers — our dad bought it for her from Ireland."

I had two lucky charms now that were supposed to keep me from harm — Gabbi's ring, and Repro's guardian angel pin. Both had failed miserably. "She gave it to me a little while ago," I said, "reckoned it would keep me safe."

"And it has," said Griff. "Here we are, safe and sound, almost back in the city. No dramas."

Yeah, no dramas. Never any dramas for me.

"Got a girlfriend?" he asked next.

"Nope," I answered, pretty quickly. I was frustrated that his question made me picture Winter's beautiful, dark eyes and wild, glittering hair. How could I think of her like that when I wasn't even sure if she was on my side? If I did have a girlfriend, I'd make sure she wasn't connected to criminals — especially not someone like Sligo who'd already tried to kill me.

Sunlight streamed through gaps in the canvas, striping our clothes and skin. Griff looked more closely at me. "I keep thinking I know you," he said.

"Join the club."

"The club?"

"People always think I'm familiar for some reason. I don't know why, and I don't get it. So anyway, what do you plan to do once we get to the city?" I asked him, avoiding the whole don't-I-know-you-from-somewhere routine.

"I'm going to live with my aunt," he said. "She wrote me a letter once. A long time ago."

"You don't sound too sure about it," I said.

He shrugged. "You can come too," he offered.

"And your aunt would be OK with that?" I doubt it, I thought to myself.

"Yeah. I reckon she'd be cool. She's young, and I'm pretty sure she lives on her own too."

"I've really gotta get to the city," I said, "and get to the hospital."

"Why? You look pretty healthy to me," Griff joked. "A bit skinny, but that's not going to kill you if you don't get there!"

"No," I said, "but it could kill my sister." My voice choked as I said the words. "She's on life support, and they're talking about switching it off."

Griff's grin faded. "Switching it off? What happened? How old is she?"

"Bushwalking fall. Nine," I said in a whisper.

"She's been in a coma for about three months. They don't think she's ever going to wake up."

"You've got to stop them!" he said.

10:49 am

We jolted along in silence for a while. I was aware of Griff glancing at me from time to time, as if he was trying to figure me out. I tightened my hold on my backpack.

2:22 pm

It had been hours since Griff and I had climbed into the back of the guy's truck we were still bumping along in. He'd stopped by the road a few times to take some phone calls and run into different stores, while we sweated it out in the back, hoping he wasn't about to grab something from the bed we were hiding in.

At one point we'd pulled into a parking lot, and he was taking so long inside this hardware store that we almost decided to make a run for it. The problem was that we were parked right outside an outdoor cafe at lunch time. Not only was it painful waiting for him to return, it was painful having to lie there under the canvas, unable to move, while the smell of coffee, burgers, pasta, and fish and chips wafted in.

Luckily for us the driver had stayed away from the back of his truck, but all the stops had meant that we were only just approaching the city outskirts — much later than we'd anticipated.

"We'd better jump out soon," I said. "I'm not sure where we are exactly, but we can't risk going too much further with this guy. We don't even know whether he's going into the city or not."

Griff nodded. "I get it — way too much country radio for one day, hey?"

"Way too much!" I agreed.

"Give me your number, Tom. And I'll call you from my aunt's."

"How about you give me yours?"

He looked at me strangely as I entered his number into my phone instead. A frown had formed on his freckled face. Then he asked the question I'd been thinking about ever since Boges had told me the news about Gabbi's life support being switched off.

"So Tom, how are you going to stop them?"

City outskirts

2:36 pm

It ended up being easy enough to jump out of the truck. We just waited for it to slow down at a red light, and then, making sure there was no traffic behind us, or anyone walking nearby, we scrambled out unnoticed. It was great timing. We watched the truck continue a couple of hundred yards up the hill before taking an exit on the left — bypassing the city entirely.

I promised myself I would stop attaching myself to moving objects. First Oriana's trunk, then Lachlan Drysdale's pickup, Melba's trunk, and then there'd been the train . . . *almost*.

2:59 pm

We'd wandered up to a place I recognized — the central markets, several miles away from town and Liberty Square, where stalls mostly sold fresh fruit, vegetables and bread.

The hospital was about a mile away, and I wanted to find somewhere that I could clean up a bit first. I wasn't sure what Griff planned on doing and when, but I definitely felt safer, and more inconspicuous, walking along beside him.

3:15 pm

My phone beeped.

 whatever u do, don't come 2 the hospital 2day.
 why?

▤ i'm there now. security everywhere. don't worry, nothing 2 do with u. some nursing protest happening. no chance u could get in.

▤ ok. thanks.

"Everything OK?" Griff asked.

"Yep, yep, just a slight change of plans."

4 APRIL

272 days to go . . .

Iron Gate Bridge

10:23 am

Repro would have to wait a little longer on the money I owed him, because Griff and I had chewed into it, finally grabbing some food last night. After Boges warned me about heavy security at the hospital, I figured we might as well have something to eat and find a place to sleep. I bought us some fruit from the market, and some kebabs from a late-night street vendor, and then we both completely crashed out on a ledge that stuck out just under the Iron Gate Bridge.

I'd only been awake for a little while and was trying to clear my head and think of an action plan for the day, when I noticed I had missed calls and a text message on my phone.

📱 CAL! WHY WON'T U ANSWER UR PHONE?! GABBI'S BEING SWITCHED OFF AT 11:30AM

THIS MORNING! A PRIEST IS ALREADY THERE. PLEASE, HURRY AND STOP THEM!!! I'VE BEGGED UR MUM NOT TO. SHE WON'T LISTEN 2 ME! U HAVE 2, CAL, DO WHATEVER IT TAKES.

10:28 am

My pulse raced as I realized that the doctors were flipping the switch in just over an hour! I felt delirious. I couldn't think.

"I have to get to the hospital," I finally said, shaking Griff awake. My panic was rising rapidly, like never before. "They're going to switch my sister off at eleven thirty! Today!"

Under the panic, my survival instincts began surfacing — instincts I didn't know I even had. There are security cameras in hospitals, something warned me. You mustn't be recognized, or you won't even make it through to Gabbi's ward, let alone save her. You need to stay cool and not get arrested before you stop them switching Gabbi off. You *must* stay cool if you want to keep her alive.

My head jerked around, looking one way, then the next.

Calm down, Cal.

Frantically, I looked around for the public bathrooms that I remembered seeing late last night.

"What's going on?" Griff slurred, still groggy with sleep.

"Gabbi! They're turning her off in— " I looked at my phone for the time, "in less than an hour!"

Griff stumbled to his feet, picked up his bag and then came after me as I headed for the bathrooms, hauling my backpack onto my shoulders as I ran.

In the dirty mirror, I saw that my hair had started growing long again. The black color had faded, leaving me with a dirty blond look.

10:43 am

As I washed my face and hands, my mind was filled with images of my sister. I felt nauseous, nearly puking in the sink. I *had* to get to her! I didn't know what I was going to do — but I had to get there to try something.

I wet my hair and slicked it straight back. Already I looked heaps different. My face seemed thinner than I remembered it too, adding to the change. The fake studs I'd once had were gone, and the tattoos I'd worn had also disappeared. I grabbed a nose ring clip out of a pocket in my bag and snapped it on with trembling fingers.

All the time, my heartbeat was drumming out: *hurry up, hurry up, hurry up.*

Griff looked on, completely confused. He had no idea what I was doing or why. He knew I had to get to the hospital, but he didn't know *who* I was. He didn't know that I had to conceal my identity or I'd be arrested . . . and Gabbi would surely die.

"I'll explain another time," I said, as I fumbled in my backpack and found a dark eye pencil that Boges had brought me when I was living in the St. John's House. Urgency was making my fingers unreliable.

My heart was now beating out, *I'm on my way, Gabs, I'm on my way, hold on for me,* as I used the pencil to thicken and darken my eyes and eyebrows.

"You sure look different," Griff said, as I swung my backpack over my shoulders and bolted out the door in the direction of the hospital.

"Good luck with your sister," he called after me. "I really hope it works out for you!"

10:56 am

I looked down at my phone for the time and then forced myself to run faster.

Saint Marie Hospital Entrance

11:14 am

All around the entrance area were security cameras.

Look calm, look calm.

A big man, wearing navy coveralls, boots, and a duty belt with a radio and baton, glanced at me as I walked through the admission doors.

I stepped up to the reception desk, terrified that I'd be recognized before I could get to my sister. I couldn't afford any delays now.

I checked the time.

11:17 am

I had only thirteen minutes left!

I had to wait for a large group of people ahead of me to quit asking the overworked receptionist stupid questions. I watched as minutes ticked away on the big clock above the entrance doors.

11:20 am

"I'm looking for Gabbi Ormond," I said hurriedly, as the receptionist was finally able to look at me. She bobbed her blonde head down to find my sister's details, then looked at something written in her notes. I was silently commanding her *hurry up, just hurry up!* She seemed to take forever.

Behind her, the tiny, hooded security camera recorded everything that was happening. I kept my head half-turned away.

"Are you a relative?" asked the nurse, looking very concerned.

I hesitated. If I hid my identity and said, "No," I probably wouldn't be allowed in to see my sister. If I said, "Yes," I'd have to give my name.

"Please," I begged, avoiding the question, "I must see her."

"I'm afraid only relatives are allowed in at this stage."

A terrible thrill of fear shot through me. "What do you mean? What do you mean by '*at this stage*?'" As afraid as I was, I still didn't believe it was true!

"I'm sorry," the nurse replied, and I could see she was really trying to be very nice to me, "but I'm not at liberty to discuss patients. You must get permission from the medical staff or her family if you want to see her."

I walked away, heart racing crazily. *At this stage,* she'd said. Was it happening already?

Were they switching it off right now? Was I too late? I would never forgive myself. Desperately, I searched every sign and bulletin board on the wall. Although I felt blind with shock, three big, white letters stood out on a sign: ICU, with an arrow pointing to the right.

Intensive Care Unit

11:25 am

Quickly, I hurried down the corridor, following the arrow to the end where I could see double doors and another sign indicating Intensive Care. A woman in a white uniform was pushing a cart along, heading for the doors. Ahead of her they opened, and a nurse, looking at his watch as he came out from the ICU ward, nodded to the woman with the cart, then walked into the men's bathroom.

I silently slipped in behind the woman with the cart. She'd turned and was heading off to the right, towards another door at the end of the long ward. I didn't know when she'd wheel back this way. Or when the nurse who was taking the bathroom break would be back. All I knew was I didn't have much time.

11:26 am

The door at the end of the ward opened, and I saw Mum.

My heart was torn. Half of me longed to run up to her, the other half wanted to scream at her: how could you think of switching Gabbi off? And how could you think I put her in the coma?

My anger almost evaporated when I saw how thin and hunched over she was, as if crushed. In the few months since I'd seen her, my happy-go-lucky, youthful, pretty mother had vanished, and in her place was this sickly-looking stranger. My blood was pounding louder than ever in my ears. I stood, indecisive.

Uncle Rafe walked into my view and put his arm around Mum. He was much grayer and thinner too, since I'd last seen him at Burger Barn with his lawyer, when I'd hidden myself from him.

I could see past Mum's bowed head to where a priest was leaning towards her, saying something to her as she wept.

Any second now and the medical people would be there to do their job.

11:28 am

I could make out four beds hidden behind

curtains. Tiptoeing, I lifted the white curtain around the first bed. An old man with his mouth open and his eyes closed lay on the pillow. I moved on to the next one and peeked in. A boy wrapped in bandages and hooked up to all sorts of drip stands lay there stiffly.

I lifted the curtain on the next bed. It was empty. Drip stands clustered at the head of the bed and two monitors showed blank, dead faces.

I felt sure this had been Gabbi's bed. What if they'd done it a little earlier than Boges had said? What if it was ten thirty, not eleven thirty? What if that was why Mum was crying, and Rafe and the priest were trying to comfort her? Had I been too late to save my little sister? I opened my mouth because I could feel a terrible scream rising up through my body. I didn't care any more about whether I was caught or not. But just before the scream hit my throat, I heard something that made the urge fade away.

Somewhere close by I could hear one of Gabbi's favorite songs from when she was really little, playing.

"All the pretty little horses," sang the voice, "blacks and bays, dapples and grays, all the pretty little horses."

It was the nursery rhyme she'd always loved when she was a baby. Mum used to sing it to her.

My fingers were trembling as I drew back the curtain around the last bed.

There was my little sister, eyes closed, her thin face almost as pale as the pillow on which she rested. A tube snaked up her nose, and her chest was rising and falling to the sound of an automatic machine. A monitor next to her was showing the slow, steady "blip" of her heartbeat. Beside her was a small CD player, softly playing the song I recognized.

I was shocked at what I saw. It was like my little sister had been hollowed out — as if only her shell was left. Mum had tied a little blue ribbon with a bow around her forehead, so she looked even younger than nine. If it hadn't been for the slow and steady rise of her chest and the electronic monitors that surrounded her, I might have even thought she was already gone.

Tears stung my eyes as I picked up her small, cold hand. I put my mouth close to her ear, willing every part of myself, my heart and my strength, into the words, "Gabbi, listen to me. It's Cal. I'm here, and I'm telling you it's not your time to go. You've gotta get better. You've gotta come around. *Please*. I didn't hurt you. We both know that. I want you to know that I'm safe. And you're safe too. I'm so sorry I haven't been in to see you until now. When you're well again, I'll explain to you why. So hurry up and get better, will you? I'll be back just as soon as I can, but I can't find out the truth about what Dad was investigating in Ireland unless I know that you're going to be all right. I can't do this without you! Tell me you're coming back! Please, Gabbi, I need you, I miss you. Tell me you're not going to die!"

Her face remained calm and still, but I could see a tiny blue vein pulsing in her temple.

I squeezed her hand even tighter. "Tell me you're not going to die! You don't have to talk. Just tell me in some way! No matter how small the movement, I'll see it. I'll get it. I promise!"

What happened next is hard to describe. Had I imagined it, or did I see her whole body somehow expand slightly — as if something rippled through her?

A voice behind me shocked me back to the reality of my dangerous situation.

"Cal!" My mother stood at the end of the bed, her eyes wide with shock. The handful of tissues she was holding dropped to the floor. "Oh,

Cal! What are you doing here? What have you done to yourself? What are you doing to Gabbi?"

"Mum," I started to say, "Mum — I had to come. I told you I was going to come. You can't do this. You can't let the doctors turn the machines off!"

I took one last look at Gabbi. Her eyelids fluttered. Definitely fluttered.

"Look! Look, there! See? Did you see that? Look! Gabbi's responding!"

My mother's hand hesitated, hovering above the red emergency button by the bed.

"Did you see that, Mum?" I repeated. "Her eyelids flickered!"

But she wasn't looking at Gabbi — she wouldn't take her eyes off *me*.

"Cal, I have to do this. I'm calling the medical staff!"

"Mum, I didn't do any of the things they said I did. You must believe me!"

I knew I had to move fast. Any moment now and the staff and security would be racing into this area.

"I'm the same Cal I've always been," I continued.

"I blame myself," she interrupted. "Something happened when you were very young — I should have told you. It's affected you, Cal."

"I don't know what you're talking about," I said. "Please, I don't care, just take a look at Gabbi — her eyes. Look! It's happening again!"

Again came that delicate flicker of her long lashes on her pale cheeks.

Mum looked quickly from me to Gabbi, then back again. But she missed the moment.

"I can't see anything," she said, her hand again moving back towards the red button. Just as she was about to press it, Rafe suddenly appeared behind her.

"No, Win, don't! There are things I want to ask before— "

But he was too late. My mother had deftly avoided his restraining arm and pressed the button. "Stop trying to protect him, Rafe. He's dangerous!"

Immediately the emergency alarm bell started ringing.

"Please, Cal," she begged. "Come home. Deal with what you need to deal with! You are my son regardless, and I love you no matter what! But I cannot protect you from the consequences of your behavior. Just come home. *Please!*"

I shouted over the deafening alarm, "How could you even *think* of switching off Gabbi's life support?"

I ripped the Celtic ring off my finger and pushed it onto Gabbi's middle finger, so that she'd know I'd been there. One day, I promised myself, I'd make my mother understand.

"You haven't been here! You haven't seen her wasting away! You haven't had to watch her suffering!" Mum shouted at me. I let go of Gabbi's hand and turned towards her.

Then I saw something terrible. Mum flinched as I moved towards her — she jumped back like she thought I was going to hit her or something! She was frightened of me! Did my own mother think I was there to *harm my sister?*

Such confused feelings swirled inside me that I thought I might explode. The pressure of the ringing alarm bells seemed to be getting louder in my ears, and the need to escape completely dominated my thinking.

I could hear running feet in the corridor beyond the double doors. The crash team was racing, responding to the alarm.

It suddenly struck me: if Gabbi dies — if they switch her off — there is no point in running. I should just hand myself in. Why run? What would be the point any more? I'd have no family left to save.

But something deep inside me said, *while*

there's life there's always hope. Live, it commanded, *and find the truth.*

That did it. I was outta there!

The tears and anger in my mother's voice faded as I skidded out of the ICU and into the corridor, straight into the team of doctors and nurses who were racing towards me, white jackets flying, stethoscopes jumping. They didn't pay any attention to me as I ducked and weaved around them.

Back down the corridor, I heard someone — a nurse — crying out. "Mrs. Ormond! Mrs. Ormond! Your daughter's responding! She just moved! She's responding! I just saw her eyelids move!"

"Win!" I heard Rafe call, "It's true! She is! It's true!"

An intense wave of joy washed over me. *She was going to be OK.* I felt so happy that tears came to my eyes. "Go Gabbi!" I yelled, out loud and triumphantly!

11:51 am

Curious faces turned to look at me as I raced past them. There was nothing I could do about the security cameras mounted on every corner, except keep my face turned away as I fled.

I was almost back at the reception area

when the alarm bells stopped ringing. The brief silence that followed was quickly shattered by a loudspeaker announcement, as monitors hanging in every corridor and waiting room suddenly came alive, flickering on, and the face of a stern, official-looking man appeared.

"Attention! Attention! This is not a test. We are experiencing a serious security breach. Do not approach this person," he commanded, as a security camera picture of me by Gabbi's bed flashed up in a box beside him on the screen. "He is a wanted criminal and is considered extremely dangerous. Staff, remain calm. Please proceed with your patients to the designated evacuation areas . . . Attention! Attention!"

I raced past the reception area and towards the big exit doors. I pushed past them, flying down the few steps as a squad car screeched to a halt at the curb almost in front of me! The cop in the passenger seat turned in my direction, and our eyes locked. Of all the cops in the city it had to be *him!* The cop who had tripped over Boges in the old St. Johns Street house, when he was trying to arrest him . . . The cop who, more importantly, I jabbed with a tranquilizer before stealing his pepper spray. This was unbelievable!

"That's him!" he yelled. "The little low-life who stuck a needle in me! He's the kid the whole state is after! Grab him!"

He fumbled with something as he climbed out of the car, giving me more time to get away.

"Stop him! Police! Don't let him get away!" he shouted into the street.

I weaved around the startled people, who really couldn't get out of my way fast enough.

Not daring to take the time to look back, I ran around a corner and kept going. My mind was whirling — thinking about Gabbi finally coming around, and seeing my mum for the first time in ages, who felt like a stranger to me. My excitement conflicted with my sadness, and now I had the panic of being chased again.

Behind me, I could hear the squad car revving up and coming after me. It was a busy street, but I was an easy target. Somehow I would have to lose them.

I made another fast left-hand turn down a side street. They switched the siren on and continued after me. I raced towards the end of the street, but then my heart sank when I saw what was ahead of me.

I'd run myself into a dead end!

A tall cyclone fence blocked my escape into

the green sports field that was behind it. The squad car was close. I had no choice. I hurled myself up the fence, got to the top, and was about to swing my leg over when my backpack slid off me and crashed down to the ground!

Everything, *all* my arsenal, was in that backpack. I made a split-second decision. I would have to go down and get it! With the squad car almost pulling up beside me, I jumped back, snatched up the bag, hurled it over the fence, then threw myself at the wire netting again.

Pepper-spray Cop was on to me like a flash!

His hands grabbed my leg — the leg that still hadn't fully recovered from the lion gash. The pain made me scream and kick out with strength I didn't know I had. I heard him yell as my kick connected with his face, and I twisted and wrenched myself free, scrambling over the top of the fence, landing heavily on the grass on the other side.

I felt like yelling *Yes!* and doing a victory dance! But I had other things on my mind. I had to get out of there. And I knew it wouldn't take them long to back up the squad car and drive around to the other side of the sports field to catch me.

I cut across the center, running as hard as I

could. Once on the other side, I had to climb over more cyclone fencing.

Just as I jumped down onto the footpath, I heard the approaching siren. No!

The cops were there already!

I looked around for a way to escape. Just a little way ahead I could see a narrow walkway. I swerved into it and kept running all the way to the other end. As I reached another corner, I glanced back to see the squad car parked in the distance at the end of the walkway. Pepper-spray Cop was jumping out of the car. But he was too far away, and too slow, to have a hope of catching me now.

8:23 pm

Since losing the cops, I'd hidden out in an empty warehouse near a small printing factory. Everything that had happened at the hospital played back in my mind, and for once I was happy thinking of Gabbi in her bed.

She was safe — at least for the time being, and I had found myself somewhere to sleep for the night. I really wanted to go back to St. Johns Street, but knew it wasn't wise. Or Repro's place would have been great. I wouldn't be able to do that until I'd somehow earned back the money I owed him.

The place I was in now was OK, but I was only going to stay until I could think of a better alternative.

I pulled my sleeping bag out, and the book in the paper bag that Melba Snipe had given me tumbled to the dusty floor.

I'd completely forgotten my promise that I'd deliver the book to her friend, Elvira. Melba had been really good to me. It was important to keep my word to her. I'll make my way there tomorrow, I decided.

5 APRIL

271 days to go . . .

9:21 am

The address Melba had given me was in a suburb that was several miles from the city — Greenaway Park, on the Canterbury River. Ages ago, back in the days when we were a family and I was a little kid, we used to go fishing there.

I pulled my hoodie around my face and headed off to keep my promise.

39 Chester Road
Greenaway Park

11:00 am

The house was a small weatherboard place, the last one left in a street by the river that was dominated now by modern mansions. Mrs. Snipe's friend obviously wasn't interested in selling her house to the developers. I placed the wrapped-up book in her mailbox as promised, then wandered to the grassy nature reserve next door that led down to the river.

The sound of gentle water lapping the edge of the riverbank was comforting — I was standing in the exact place that Dad and I, and often Boges, used to come years ago to decide where to drop a line in. That was back when Boges and I were little, before Dad bought the boat Rafe and I had lost in Treachery Bay, and when all the houses on Chester Road were just like Elvira's. Most of the time we'd fish from the jetty alongside locals and, occasionally, some serious anglers.

11:18 am

The jetty was still there, crouched over the water. It looked a little worse for wear. Its piers were rotting, and there was a distinct tilt to one side. But what caught my attention was the old blue boathouse at the bottom of Elvira's backyard.

Built on the riverbank, it reached some way over the water. I slid down the bank to take a closer look, stepping onto the narrow timber deck that ran along one side of it.

Cautiously, I stepped up to the peeling, four-paneled door, and rubbed a dusty window to peer in. Through the cobwebs on the other side, I checked out the gloomy interior. There was no boat in there, although I could see the dark water rippling where one might once have bobbed, sheltered from the elements.

With a twist of the old-fashioned brass doorknob and a bit of a kick, the door opened and let me inside. I looked around first to make sure no one was watching, but I needn't have worried. The river was deserted, and the rise of the land behind me would have made it very hard for anyone to see me from any of the houses.

I eased my backpack off my right shoulder, wincing at the stinging pain that still mysteriously came and went. The floorboards, although uneven and in some places pretty iffy-looking, seemed quite capable of taking my weight. The boathouse had flooring to the halfway point, ending in a step down to the water where a boat could be moored. A narrow ledge of flooring continued on each side of the dark, slow-moving water, and two old timber gates hung slightly open, over the river.

High, dusty shelving lined the walls, and a workbench held a couple of paint cans, a pair of Wellington boots, and an ancient life jacket.

Several rusty gaff hooks hung from the ceiling, alongside a mess of fishing paraphernalia — old reels, rods and nets. The best thing I could see was a light bulb hanging down, plugged into an outlet over the bench. I switched it on, and the old bulb flickered for a second before pinging out. That was fine by me. I wouldn't have dared to put the light on during the night anyway, but I was stoked to have electricity. There was a deep sink for cleaning too, and when I turned the tap on, the pipes knocked around for a bit, and then a trickle of rusty water came out, finally running clear.

I had power and running water, under cover. Seeing as I wanted to stay near Gabbi until I had more news, I'd found my new home.

12 APRIL

264 days to go . . .

The boathouse
Greenaway Park

4:45 pm

I'd spent the whole week taking it easy, trying to rest up and straighten my head out. I really needed to see Boges — it had been ages since we'd caught up — but he'd been finding it impossible to leave his house safely since my appearance at the hospital. I left him a message telling him that I was in the old blue boathouse where we used to go fishing with Dad.

I hoped he'd come soon and bring me some more supplies, because I was almost out of everything: money, food, batteries. The batteries were running really low in my small radio, but I'd managed to hear my name back in the breaking news again, this time with a new and horrible allegation — that I'd attempted to harm my sister as she lay helpless in the hospital. Funny they should make that claim, when the doctors were about to switch her off anyway!

And Boges still hadn't even seen the Riddle! I desperately needed his thoughts on it, to help me make some sort of progress with it ... Repro and I had gone to so much trouble to steal it from Oriana, and it had pretty much just sat in the back of my bag, like nothing but gibberish, ever since. I was really wasting a lot of time, but didn't know what to do about it.

Thoughts of Gabbi being alive and starting to show signs of improvement buoyed me along. I hoped so bad that she'd heard everything I'd whispered to her in the short time I'd been alone with her.

The days were getting shorter, and I was starting to wonder what a cold winter would be like in the boathouse. I wasn't looking forward to it, but was prepared to stick it out a bit longer. When the wind came up it blew hard, whistling through the cracks, and when it rained, the ceiling leaked quite heavily. No matter how much I tried to deny it, this place was going to be miserable once the weather got cold. It made me think about where Griff Kirby was, and whether he'd had any luck with that aunt he was counting on.

I'd fixed the side door, jamming it shut with a wedge of wood. If anyone tried to come in, I could either dive into the water and swim away through the rotting wooden gates, or I could escape through the window on the other side and be off along the banks before they could reach me. I'd also moved most of the junk from the bench and made my own kind of workstation under the light of the window.

Some of the time I spent studying the words of the Riddle, reading it over and over, trying to make sense of it, wondering what had happened to the last two lines, and where it fit in with the drawings. I couldn't find any connections. I pored over Oriana's legal documents too, freaking out at the thought of the crazy guy's December 31st warning ringing true. A couple of times I considered calling Winter, thinking she might be able to help. I knew she was smart. But if the answer to the Riddle was given in the last two lines, we would have to track them down. Without them, we'd never figure it out.

15 APRIL

261 days to go . . .

8:23 pm

📱 dude, u ok? so sorry i haven't been by. way, way 2 hard. gab's the same. blinking, but not much else. stay positive.

📱 boges! i'm cool. feel like i'm wasting time, but what else can i do? thx 4 update on gab. would b good 2 see u soon. when u can.

📱 working on it. be there soon as.

📱 i have the riddle, by the way.

📱 what?! ok, soon as, i promise.

19 APRIL

257 days to go . . .

3:12 pm

As the days went by, I began to get really worried about Boges. It had been ages since I'd seen him; it was the longest time he'd left me on my own since this whole crazy thing began. Why did he have to lie *so* low? Was he in trouble — accessory after the fact or something? I was sure there were laws against helping people on the run. 🔋 everything ok, boges?

4:01 pm

Finally, my phone rang and I snatched it up.

"Boges! Where you been?"

"I know, dude — long time no talk. I'm sorry. I'm fine, how about you, more importantly? You're living in the old boathouse?"

"Yep, it's pretty small, but it's quiet enough around here for me to go unseen. So what's been happening?" I asked. "I've kinda been imagining all sorts of reasons why you haven't been able to get out to meet me."

"Nah, look, I've just been staying home and being a *good boy* — going to school, doing my homework, helping out my mum. *Your* mum, by the way, is looking heaps better. She said Gabbi's eyes focused on her a few nights ago! I think that whatever you did at the hospital worked. Gab's responding to voices and touch. Nothing much, so don't get too excited, but it's just enough to stop all that talk of *no hope*."

I felt a huge surge of relief. It felt so good that I wanted to yell.

"Although," added Boges, "some of the doctors are saying it's just an automatic response."

"Like they said about my dad," I said, "but we both know they weren't 'automatic responses.' Dad was trying to talk." I thought briefly of Jennifer Smith — she knew that Dad communicated through his eyes.

"You know, I didn't for a second believe," Boges began, "that you left that farmer guy to drown, trapped under his truck."

"*What*? Of course I didn't!"

"It was all over the news a couple of weeks ago. They said you left some guy trapped and unconscious under his pickup truck — underwater or something."

"I held his head out, to stop him from drowning! Then I left him in the hands of the police!"

"Nobody mentioned that part, but I figured as much. Anyway, this Lachlan guy hasn't said anything about you, so don't worry, only that you seemed like a good, quiet kid. They always say that, don't they?" Boges laughed for a second. "So things have eased off here a bit now, but until I'm sure it's safe I think it's best I stay prudent."

Boges is the only guy I know who uses words like "prudent."

"The cops took my cell phone again," said Boges. "But it's OK, they still don't know about this one. And that guy's been back too. You know, the one in the silver car?"

"The one who'd been sitting outside your house? The big guy who wears the turtleneck and suit jacket?" I recalled him telling me to get lost that day in Memorial Park.

"That's him. He's been outside my place constantly lately — I see him on my way to school and on the way home again. I even spotted him outside Art in the middle of a class last week! That's really why you haven't seen me lately. If Winter Frey could follow me to your old place, anyone could follow me to your new one. I don't want to give them any extra help finding you. I just can't take the risk with him hanging around."

I hated that he was right, but tried not to think about it. "Have you been keeping an eye on my blog?" I asked, changing the subject. "I've gotta say, I've hardly thought about it, but the lies the media keeps reporting about me, painting me like a monster, makes me want to get online and set the record straight."

"Look, don't worry too much about it, OK? We'll jump on my laptop as soon as I can come around. Anyway, on to more important things: you have the Riddle!"

"Sure do!" I grinned when I heard Boges's excited intake of breath down the line. Last time I was about to tell him about it, he'd taken over the conversation to tell me about Gabbi.

"You're serious, the actual Riddle, from Oriana's?"

"That's right. Here with me now," I said, thinking about the missing two final lines, but I figured I'd fill him in on that later. "*Plus* I've got some legal letters about the Ormond Singularity that I think you could help me with."

"Dude, I'll be down on the river before you know it! Don't keep me in suspense. Tell me the Riddle, read it to me. What does it say?"

"Hey," I laughed, "hang on." I reached for my bag and lifted the Riddle out from the folder. Boges listened in silence as I read it to him, stumbling a little over the unfamiliar words.

The ORMOND RIDDLE

Eight are the Leaves on my Ladyes Grace

Fayre sits the Rounde of my Ladyes Face

Thirteen Teares from the Sunnes grate Doore

Make right to treadde in Gules on the Floore

But adde One in for the Queenes fayre Sinne

Then alle shall be tolde and the Yifte unfold

"Dude, that is going to take some figuring out," Boges said, after letting it sink in. "As soon as it's safe, I'll be there with the laptop. We've got to stay on the program. Remember what we're after in this mess. Your dad's secret. The DMO. We've got to crack this."

He was right again. I couldn't do any more for Gabbi now that she'd shown some improvement, so I'd just have to put it behind me for the time being, and get on with the drawings, the Singularity and the Ormond Riddle. I still wasn't sure I wanted to run off to Mount Helicon just yet, even though it was probably more important than ever to try for information from Great-uncle Bartholomew.

"Cal, I've gotta get back to my studying before Mum starts hounding me. Just wait till you see what I'm working on for you," he said, as he tapped something metallic. "I'm calling it 'Disappearing Dust.'"

"Disappearing Dust? What's that?"

"Wait and see, dude, wait and see."

23 APRIL

253 days to go . . .

Greenaway Park stores

1:16 pm

Wearing my hat low, and trying to look as ordinary as possible, I'd wandered to the Greenaway Park stores to grab some food and stuff to take back to the boathouse. I hadn't been anywhere in days and had no choice but to venture out to restock. I couldn't wait any longer for Boges.

There was a new-looking high school across the road from the short row of stores. It had large sports fields and lots of shady trees with benches under them. A pang of sadness went through me as I thought of those carefree days, with me and Boges messing around at school, kicking a ball around on the grass, getting up to mischief with one of his new inventions crawling around the floor at the back of the classroom.

A group of kids was coming out of the school gates, laughing and talking, and I envied them. Even though they were the ones who spent their time shut up behind the school gates every day, *I* was the one in a prison. They were free — free of fear and the worry of where they'd sleep each night, or whether they'd be able to find anything to eat or drink . . . Free from the constant threat of the cops, or Vulkan Sligo and Oriana de la Force and their thugs coming after them . . . Free to just get on with their lives.

I was about to pass them by and turn my head away, when I saw one of them staring hard at me.

I stared back, frozen with shock! It was him! My double! The kid that looked exactly like me!

For a second our eyes engaged, and it seemed like an electric shock jolted between us. He quickly grabbed the guy beside him, and I watched the stunned expression on his face as he pointed his friend in my direction. I couldn't stick around, waiting for a whole bunch of school kids to start gawking at me. And clearly I was still recognizable.

I was off, head down, sprinting away from the stores and Greenaway Park. I would have to stay away from the boathouse until it was dark.

Who *was* this kid? I asked myself again. Was he real? Why did he look like me? Was I hallucinating? I knew the mind could do funny things — I'd seen my own dad go through it. But this was real, surely. I *had* seen him. And he had seen me.

24 APRIL

252 days to go . . .

1:01 am

My double had not left my mind since I'd seen him in the afternoon. Now it was dark, late, and I was curled up, restless and unable to get to sleep.

A sudden thought hit me: what if he was the one that attacked Gabbi and Uncle Rafe? That could explain why Rafe thought it was me! It explained everything! Of course my uncle would have thought it was me. He'd just made a mistake!

That was if the kid was real and not some product of my crazy mind . . . and what would he get out of murdering the family of another kid that looked like him?

I laughed at myself and my ridiculous thoughts.

It was true that Rafe wasn't my most favorite person in the world — he'd created a lot of problems for me — nearly getting us both drowned in Treachery Bay, taking that package that was addressed to me, saying he thought I was the one that shot him that dreadful day at home in Richmond.

I wasn't real happy about him getting too close to my mother, either. After all, I couldn't forget the fact that he'd hired a private detective to look for me. Right now, this very minute, someone in the city could very well be trying to track me down, by asking questions, hanging around places they thought I might show up, talking to old school friends . . . just like Bruno — Red Tank Top — had been doing at the bus depot.

An image of Rafe trying to stop Mum from pressing the emergency alarm back at the hospital flashed into my mind. He'd tried to stop her so I could get away.

1:20 am

I felt very alone. Apart from Boges, there was no one I could really rely on. And even Boges hadn't exactly been there for me lately, although I understood why. I thought briefly of Winter Frey and how sometimes she appeared to be an ally, but other times I was convinced she was a rat. I'd met some good people: Lachlan Drysdale and Melba Snipe, for instance. Even Griff turned out to be OK.

I wondered how Repro, another of my new friends, was doing. I'd spent just about all of the money I'd been trying to keep for him. I hoped that he was all right.

Some days I felt enthusiastic and keen to get on with the quest to find the truth. But other days, like this one, were bad — I felt lonely and miserable, missing Mum and Gabbi and Dad. The old days, when we were a family together, seemed to come from another lifetime.

25 APRIL

251 days to go . . .

Memorial Park

5:45 am

It wasn't just loneliness and restlessness that drove me into the city. I'd been having another sleepless night, tossing and turning, and was drawn back to the image of the Angel in the stained glass window.

I felt strangely safe and anonymous in the gray, early morning, standing in the light drizzle in Memorial Park, a short distance away from the cenotaph. A gentle, misty rain made halos around the park lights. Maybe there was something I'd missed, I thought. Maybe there was something there that I hadn't yet noticed that would be a clue — maybe something that would lead to solving the Ormond Riddle.

I wondered if Dad had ever seen this Angel. If he'd known about it, he might have started asking questions back home, rather than in Ireland. Maybe if he'd done that, he'd still be alive today.

6:10 am

The interior was still fairly dark, as the sun had not yet begun to rise. Even so, a couple of people stood talking quietly on the steps near the rusty gates. As I passed them on my way towards the entrance door, I saw there was another guy in there, in jogging gear, with his back to me, staring up at the Angel.

I was about to move up and stand behind him, when I realized who it was.

He sensed my presence and swung around to look at me.

It was Rafe!

"Cal! What are you doing here?" he asked, completely taken aback.

He stepped closer to me, and I couldn't read his expression in the dim light, but it was light enough for me to see him pull out his phone.

"How do you know it's me?" I asked, urgently. "There's another guy around the place who looks exactly like me. I could be him."

Rafe looked at me as if I was crazy. "Cal, what are you saying? Are you OK? Son, you're not making any sense. Why are you here? In the cenotaph?"

"I could ask you the same thing. What do you want with the Ormond Angel?"

"You mean this?" he asked, pointing to the stained glass window. "I only just heard about it, and thought I'd jog by to check it out. Why, Cal?"

"How did you hear about it?" I asked.

"Why did you suggest that there might be someone else that looks like you, Cal? What made you think of such a crazy idea?"

My uncle's face was very still and watchful. He looked scared of me. He flipped open his phone.

"Who are you calling?" I asked, as he punched a number and raised it to his ear.

"Your mother, of course," he said. "Now that I've found you, you must come home with me. There are a lot of questions you need to answer."

"I don't think so," I said, picturing myself being questioned in a jail cell. "I've gotta go," I said, backing away.

Rafe reached out his other hand to restrain me. "Please, Cal. Listen to reason."

"Tell Mum I love her," I shouted out, as I ducked away, spun around, and broke into a run.

I heard him shout after me as I ran, pulling my hoodie down over my head.

He was coming after me, calling my name as he ran. Within a few moments, a couple of other people had joined him, and I could hear them shouting, "It's him! The Psycho Kid! Call the police!"

What was I going to do? I knew I could lose my pursuers on foot, but cop cars would be flooding the area any second. I was too far from the boathouse. *And my backpack!*

The shouts died down as I left Rafe and the others behind. But I had to go to ground. Find somewhere quiet to hide until the noise died down. My wild running had brought me fairly close to the railway yards. I kept running until I came to the fence around the disused railway buildings.

Not far from here there were three old steel filing cabinets, standing against a stone wall . . .

Repro's lair

6:53 am

I banged on the central cabinet. "Repro! Repro! Let me in! It's me! It's Cal!"

Behind me I could hear the sound of sirens,

screaming as they searched for me.

I banged again, harder. "Please, Repro! Let me in. I'm in trouble—" I started to say, then thought better of it. "I've got your money!"

The back of the filing cabinet suddenly snapped open, and I tumbled through. Equally suddenly, it snapped back into place, and Repro grabbed my arm to stop me from falling flat on my face. I gasped, tripping over one of the rickety chairs near his collection. I threw myself forwards, panting and catching my breath.

"Well, give it up!" he said, dancing around in his nimble, skinny way, tugging down the jacket of his green suit and rubbing his hands together. "Come on, you didn't wake me up for nothing, did ya?"

"Oh, sorry," I said, forgetting how early it was.

"Get your breath, and I'll get you a drink of water," he said, before wandering over to the sink.

He came back with a glass of water, which I gulped down gratefully, and sat himself down at his cluttered table. He observed me with his pale, possum eyes.

"OK, down to business. Where's the money?"

Finally I was able to straighten up and finish off the water. The muscles in my legs stopped burning, and my heart rate slowed down.

"Repro, it's like this. The situation I find myself in is something like your Singapore martial arts championship."

Repro frowned. "But I didn't win the martial arts championship."

"Exactly. You said you *would have* won it, if you'd gone to it."

"Meaning?"

"Meaning I *would have* had the money for you, if I hadn't already spent it."

I watched his frown deepen, his cheeks sharpen and pale, and his mouth become a thin line. Angry flickers around his eyes told me I was in for an earful.

I braced myself, ready for it.

But it didn't happen. His face relaxed, and he threw his head back and burst out laughing. "You rascal! You cheeky rascal! *Like my martial arts championship, eh?* Something similar, eh?"

He stopped laughing and moved closer, enquiring with his eyes, suddenly serious. "Have you got any money at all?"

"Not really," I said lamely. "But I still have every intention of paying you for helping me out. I just haven't had much luck lately getting that organized. You saved my butt that day at

Oriana's. Last time I saw you, you were yelling at me to jump out the window while that skinny stooge Kelvin was coming at you through the door. How did you end up getting out of there?"

"He got a lucky hold on me and was about to knock my lights out when I suddenly kicked him and head-butted him in the same movement. I call it my 'double horse kick maneuver.' I learned it when I was in . . . never mind where I learned it. Did that make him cranky! He let go a little and that gave me time to spring out of his grasp and scramble out the window." Repro demonstrated his moves dramatically as he spoke, sending a couple of his collection towers toppling.

A noise outside made me jump. "What was that?" I hissed.

Both of us froze, turning our attention to the outside world. I became aware of the thumping of a helicopter and sirens coming closer. I heard feet running past the frail cover of the rusting filing cabinets. If they bash through that line of defense, I thought, we're dead. Nowhere to run, nowhere to hide. Had I brought danger to Repro again?

The feet moved away.

A few moments more, and everything was

quiet again.

"You said there was another way here," I reminded Repro. "You said there were two tunnels?"

He shook his head. "No, no, no. Way too dangerous. Way too dangerous."

"What's the problem?" I asked.

He started pulling a bookcase away from the back wall. "Come see for yourself."

Moving the bookcase had revealed the opening of a tunnel, about the size of a small fireplace. I peered into it. There was nothing but blackness.

"I can't see anything."

Repro pushed the bookcase back. "That's because it's blocked. Dangerous rock falls. The tunnel had to be abandoned even while the original work was being done. That's why I've never used it. So anyway," Repro said, changing the subject back to his escape from Oriana's place. "It was sheer artistry on my part. Do you know the advice of Sun Tzu, the great general of ancient China?"

I had to admit that I didn't have a clue who he was talking about.

"I've learned a lot from him, as well as from the street and my martial arts training.

The general's advice worked perfectly with that hot-headed clown back at Oriana's place!" chuckled Repro. "*If the enemy is hot-tempered and irrational, enrage him,*" he recited. "And that's why I mocked and laughed at him from the window before I left!"

Repro squatted and made a ridiculous face and waved his fingers around his head.

I nodded, understanding. When a person is hot-tempered and irrational to begin with, more provocation can only make him worse, and therefore they are much more likely to make a mistake.

"He came at me running, just about busting out of his clothes with rage, just dying to get his ugly paws on me. But I skipped sideways, out onto the tree, and he went sailing through the window! I was fine, clinging onto the branch beside the window while he crashed straight down. Not quite straight down, actually. He went through the roof of the garden shed, which broke his fall and probably saved his neck. It was a very satisfactory outcome . . . for me. So while he was wailing and carrying on down there, pulling broken bits of potted plants out of his hair, I scrambled down the sensible way, using the tree and the drainpipes, and was back here safe and sound with my collection, probably before he was even up on his legs again."

"Awesome," I said, and I meant it.

10:01 am

I filled Repro in on what I'd been up to since we last saw each other, and I promised that I would pay him for his help in keeping Oriana de la Force's thugs off my back that time.

"You must be on to something very big," he said, "to have those sorts of heavies after you. Plus Vulkan Sligo. Must be worth a lot," he added, looking at me slyly.

"I've gotta live long enough first," I said, standing up, ready to leave. "Thanks for letting me in, especially after lying to you. You probably saved me from being arrested."

"Maybe you'll be a rich man one day, Cal Ormond," he said. "Just don't forget me then." He gave his cheesy grin, and the possum eyes shone with mischief as I slipped out through the cabinet.

26 APRIL

250 days to go . . .

The boathouse
Greenaway Park

10:32 pm

Back at the boathouse, I'd been lucky with a fishing rod I'd hooked up and had caught a couple of redfin perch. There were plenty of carp, but you'd have to be desperate to eat them. And I wasn't quite that desperate.

I'd made a frying pan out of the bottom of a large can and fried up my fish on a small campfire beside the boathouse. It was a good little fire and didn't smoke much at all.

As I waited for the small fish to cook, I thought about Rafe at the cenotaph. I also thought again of the strange words Mum had said to me back at the hospital. Something about telling me what had happened when I was very young . . . what had she meant by that?

I didn't even know if the "something" that had "happened" had happened to me, or to someone else in the family. Had something dreadful happened when I was little, like a house invasion or a fire? Or a car accident? What had she meant? It had sounded like something that she thought was responsible for me going crazy and hurting my uncle and my sister. Had she dropped me on my head?! Had the legacy of whatever had happened made me more likely to see things that weren't there?

I carried the cooked fish back into the boathouse and ate them straight out of the pan. They tasted so good, but I couldn't ignore the horrible feeling in my stomach — I needed answers, and I needed them bad. There were too many secrets in my family. Too many things hidden away. Whatever Dad had uncovered in Ireland was casting long and dangerous shadows over me. And what did Rafe know about the Ormond Angel?

Like Repro had said, whatever it was, it had to be big. And Mum's words puzzled and intrigued me. Was she implying that the long and dangerous shadows had been there all along, from when I was little? Did she — and maybe Rafe — know something about me that I didn't know?

28 APRIL

248 days to go . . .

7:21 pm

▯ if all's clear, i'll b there in the morning.

▯ great! c u then. just b careful who's around b4 u come down to the river.

▯ will do. cya. can't wait 2 c riddle.

29 APRIL

247 days to go . . .

9:10 am

I was wiping dust away from the boathouse bench, waiting for Boges to show up, when my phone rang.

I knew the voice right away.

"Hey, Cal," she said. "How are you, stranger?"

There is such a thing as a happy shock, which is what Winter had just given me. It's quite different from a bad shock. But it's still a shock.

"Hey," I said, "I was just thinking of you a little while ago."

"Good," she said. "Well, I *hope* it's good — really depends on what were you thinking."

"Yeah," I said, "I guess." I couldn't exactly tell her what had been on my mind — that I didn't fully trust her, but I was willing to take a risk. "Do you mean," I asked, "what was I thinking when I was thinking of you a while ago? Or what I think about what you just said just then?"

I shut up suddenly. I was raving like a moron. Her giggle floated down the line and made me feel funny — a mixture between embarrassed and wanting to laugh out loud.

"Not sure I followed all that," she said. "Maybe I better tell you what *I'm* thinking."

"Yep, do that," I said with relief.

"Actually, I'll tell you what I'm *not* thinking first. I'm not thinking that you left a man to drown in a creek."

"Of course I didn't."

"I'm also not thinking that you went to the hospital to try and hurt your sister."

"Right again," I said, relieved to hear from another person who knew I wasn't out to harm anyone.

I knew that Boges was on his way, and I felt awkward because I knew he didn't trust Winter. And yet she was smart — maybe she could help with solving the Ormond Riddle.

"It would be cool if I knew where you were right now," she said, "because if I did, maybe you would invite me to join you? We could have something to eat. Listen to music. Just sorta hang out. My tutor isn't coming today. So what do you think? Where are you now?"

I hesitated for a second. "I found a new place. It's an old boathouse. Down on the riverbanks, in the backyard of the house that I guess owns it. I don't think anyone's been near the place in years. Besides me," I added.

Winter took down the address, and I explained to her how to find it. Like I'd said to Boges, I warned her about coming in quietly and unseen. I didn't want old Elvira noticing the new tenants in her boathouse.

"So when are you coming?" I asked.

"Soon!" was all she said, before hanging up. I didn't know what to make of her. Maybe she liked me. Maybe not. I wanted so bad to be able to trust her, but all I could say was that she confused me.

9:31 am

I heard someone outside and froze. When a careful glance out of the dusty window revealed who it was, I quickly opened the door.

"Boges!" I said, so happy to see my friend.

"Man, this is cool!" he said, as he carefully stepped inside and looked around. "You've got yourself a waterfront property! Oh, so fancy," he added, walking over and turning on the faucet and trying the light. "Even an indoor swimming pool," he added, indicating the dark water that gurgled at the river end of the boathouse. "It's weird to be back near the river after such a long time."

Boges had come with plenty of good stuff for me — canned soup, bread, ham, biscuits, nuts, energy bars, chips, bottled water and a few more chocolate bars. From the very bottom of his bag he drew out a cool little electric hot plate that he'd retrieved from a dumpster.

"All it took was a bit of fiddling with the wiring," he said proudly, setting it down on the counter after clearing some space for it among the jars of fish hooks and dusty reels. "Works perfectly now."

He switched it on to demonstrate, and very soon the coil of the hot plate glowed a dull red.

"Thanks, Boges," I said. "That's awesome. I cooked myself up some fish the other night, but was a little worried about the smoke. This," I pointed to the hot plate, "is perfect. I don't know how I'm ever going to repay you for all this stuff."

"Leave that to me," laughed Boges. "There are quite a few jobs I'm going to be calling you in on. Like painting the ceiling at *our* house. It's even worse than this place."

"When I crack the Ormond Riddle, find out the secret my dad was on to, and become rich and famous, maybe I'll be able to pay someone to do it for you!"

"You never know!" Boges laughed. "Now, my friend, show me the Ormond Riddle!"

Carefully, I lifted the soft parchment out of its sleeve in the folder in my backpack and handed it to him. He had already pulled out a pen and his battered little notebook with the rubber band around it.

"Wicked! Here it actually is!" he said, scratching his head. "The Ormond Riddle!"

I listened while Boges read it aloud.

Boges lifted his head from his reading and looked at me. "Nothing's coming to me . . . *yet*. Have you had any brilliant ideas?"

"First thing I should tell you," I said, "is that there are only six lines here, not eight. You can see where it looks like the last two lines have been cut off."

Boges looked more closely at the paper's edges and frowned. "You're right. Someone's cut this, for sure. That's not going to make it any easier. But I guess that was the idea. Actually, I can tell you one thing. Gules."

"Gules? What about it?"

"It means 'red' in heraldry," he said, as he scribbled in his notebook.

"Sorry, but I don't speak *heraldry*," I said.

"Heraldry," Boges repeated, "is the study of families and their shields — like the Ormond shield."

"There's an Ormond shield?" I asked.

Boges whisked through the photographs on his phone until he found the one he was looking for. "Here it is. I got it off the Net. It might be helpful."

It was divided into four quarters, two of them red, with what looked like eggs in cups on them. I pointed to the red bits of the shield. "So that's *gules*," I said. "OK, now all we have to do is figure out the rest of it."

Boges turned his attention back to the Riddle and read it again.

"This is going to require all my brain capacity," he sighed, tucking the notebook back in his pocket. "So let's get all the drawings out again. Maybe if we put everything together — the drawings and the Riddle — and study them as a group, something will make sense. I think I also need some serious brain food. Give me one of those chocolates I brought, will ya?"

I tossed him one, which he tore open and then snapped in two. He passed the smaller piece to me.

While Boges sorted through the drawings, I filled him in about what happened at the hospital, and also back in the country. I told him all about being run off the road by the monster SUV driven by Kelvin and Sumo, and having to hold Lachlan's head above water so that he wouldn't drown. I told him about my crazy night in the bush in the middle of a live fire exercise, with bullets whistling past my head, and the sumo wrestler tracking me down and getting himself wounded in the crossfire. What a stroke of luck that was.

I told him about stowing away in the back of Mrs. Snipe's car, and how she'd known all along I was there, and instead of freaking out and calling the cops, invited me in for dinner. And lastly I told him about meeting Griff Kirby, the guy who woke me up while trying to steal my bag.

Boges grinned and made a joke of it. "What is it about you? Ending up in the trunks of women's cars?"

I looked up from the last drawing, hesitant about what I was going to say next. I didn't want Boges to think I was cracking up. But I had to tell him.

"Boges, I saw that kid again," I said, "the one that looks — or used to look — like the spitting image of me."

"Where?" he asked.

"Not far from here. I was on my way to the store because I'd run out of food. He was coming out of the Greenaway Park high school. We eyeballed each other. But I took off because he was pointing me out to a friend of his. He was just as shocked as I was."

Boges stared at me in silence.

"I tell you, Boges. I *know* what I saw. It was *him*."

"You're telling me you saw the guy who looks *exactly* like you?"

"He's heavier than me, and looks a lot . . . healthier than I do."

"And he just keeps turning up all of a sudden? How can you be so sure?"

Now, some time after, I had to admit that I didn't know how I could be so sure.

"Boges, I reckon he'd be trying to change his appearance too. He wouldn't want to be going around looking like the State's Most Wanted! He must know that he looks like the Psycho Kid. People must give him a hard time about it all the time!"

But who was he really? I wondered.

I went on to explain to Boges my latest theory — that maybe the look-alike kid had attacked Gabbi and Rafe, and that was why they thought *I* was responsible.

Boges considered this for a while. "I just don't see why some total stranger, even if he does look like you . . ." I could see Boges was not remotely convinced. "There's got to be a motive," he continued. "Human beings don't do things without a reason. Even crazy things — there's always a reason — even if it's the voices in their head."

"The look-alike kid could have a reason — if he did it. We just don't know about it yet."

"I don't think so, Cal," Boges said firmly, before turning back to the drawings.

Even Boges with his supercharged brainpower had to admit defeat. He couldn't find any strong connections. He threw down the pen he'd been holding. "I'm not making any sense of it," he said. "But I'll take it home with me and keep working on it." He took a shot of it with his cell phone.

"Now, let's do something about your blog," he said, opening his laptop and turning it to face me.

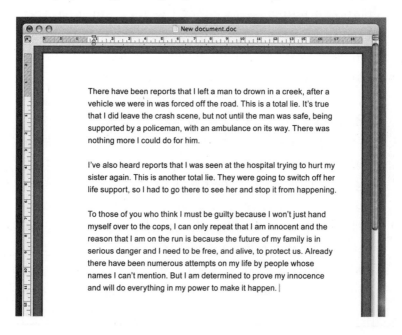

There have been reports that I left a man to drown in a creek, after a vehicle we were in was forced off the road. This is a total lie. It's true that I did leave the crash scene, but not until the man was safe, being supported by a policeman, with an ambulance on its way. There was nothing more I could do for him.

I've also heard reports that I was seen at the hospital trying to hurt my sister again. This is another total lie. They were going to switch off her life support, so I had to go there to see her and stop it from happening.

To those of you who think I must be guilty because I won't just hand myself over to the cops, I can only repeat that I am innocent and the reason that I am on the run is because the future of my family is in serious danger and I need to be free, and alive, to protect us. Already there have been numerous attempts on my life by people whose names I can't mention. But I am determined to prove my innocence and will do everything in my power to make it happen.

I read out what I'd written to Boges, and he nodded with approval. "Sounds good, man. I'll upload it as soon as I can get to an internet cafe," he promised. "Nothing personal, dude, but I don't want anything related to you anywhere on my system."

"Thanks," I said. "Hey, you were going to tell me about something called 'Disappearing Dust?'"

"Aha," he grinned widely, "it's a work in progress. I think it'll come in handy to a guy on the run. I won't say any more. My first test was quite successful, but Mum's forbidden me to test it in the house again after the incident with the Fire Department."

"What in the world is it?" I asked, intensely curious now.

Boges shook his head, mischievously. "Now let's have another look at the Riddle."

"Don't move," I hissed to Boges, as a noise outside approached. Creeping to the window, flat against the wall, I took a peek.

Winter Frey stood there on the riverbank, frowning up at the boathouse, her eyes dark, as always, and something red and black sparkled in her hair. Silver bracelets jangled as she moved her shoulder bag from one side, flung it over the other, and put a hand on her hip.

She stepped up to the window and knocked softly.

I ignored Boges's groaning and opened the door for her. She swept inside with the breeze.

Boges started furiously grabbing up the drawings and the Riddle. "You asking for trouble?" he muttered.

"I've got very important information to tell you," Winter said to me, but when she saw what Boges was doing, packing away the drawings and the parchment with the Riddle text on it, she stepped over to him.

"What are you doing? Don't take that away! That's new! Let me see!" she said, slinging her shoulder bag beside the workbench.

Boges hesitated, and Winter went straight for the Riddle, picking it up delicately, mesmerized by it.

"Oh, wow! What is this gorgeous thing?" she asked.

Boges looked at me, then at Winter. He was watchful and frowning, the frustration in his eyes obvious, his mouth a narrow, disapproving line, the two deepening lines on his forehead indicating deep concern.

"I've never seen this stuff," she said, touching

the soft, strange fabric on which the Riddle was written, "I've only read about it. This soft stuff it's written on," she said, gently patting it, "is called vellum."

"Vellum?" I asked.

"It's calf or lamb skin," Boges added shortly after. "Used for very important documents in the old days." Winter made a face at him as he was turned to me, before starting to read the Riddle.

"That's beautiful," she breathed, looking up at us both. I could see she was impressed. "It's got your name on it. Like the Ormond Angel." She flashed me an excited look. "Where did you get it?"

"None of your business," snapped Boges.

"Charming, as always," Winter snapped back at Boges, with a flick of her hair.

"Um . . . I sort of borrowed it," I said vaguely, "from the person who had it before me."

"Where from? And from whom?"

This was getting awkward. I didn't want to lie to her straight out. "From a legal person who's — who's very interested in our family," I added, thinking that was at least partly true of Oriana de la Force.

"You *are* being secretive," she said. "Never mind. I'll find out in good time. Secrets are my specialty."

"And *that*'s no secret," Boges muttered.

Winter gave him a withering look and put the Riddle down very gently, as if it was something very precious — and I suppose it was, except it didn't make any sense. Then she dug through her bag and brought out some chocolates. She smiled and said, "Isn't anyone going to offer me a drink?"

11:12 am

I could see that Boges was not at all happy about her presence. He hadn't said anything in a while — and usually he had plenty to say. He kept giving me dirty looks, every look demanding, *What's she doing here?*

Winter sipped room temperature water out of a jar — all I had to offer her. "I don't understand why you want to keep your secret from me," she said. She looked at Boges, as if in an effort to convince him. "He wouldn't have even found that Angel without me. I could help him even more, you know."

Boges poked a stick in the dirt, next to where he was sitting on the ledge over the water.

"I love riddles," Winter said, from where she now stood near the doorway, "and I'm great at figuring out secrets — and knowing when people are telling lies."

"Well, aren't you just great at everything," mumbled Boges. "And you're full of lies yourself."

"I heard that!"

"You were supposed to," he said. "Does your boss know where you are today?"

"No one's the boss of me, nerd boy."

The way she said "nerd boy" would have stripped paint from the walls — if there'd been any in this old boathouse.

"That's not what I heard."

"Then your big ears heard wrong, *right?*"

"*Wrong.* My big ears heard right. You think Vulkan Sligo's just lovely company? I don't think so."

"Hey, Boges," I said uneasily, "maybe Winter has her reasons for that."

"I'm sure she has," he said. "Sligo's probably on his way here right now. Or at least his goons are."

"You don't know anything," said Winter. "Cal can trust me. I don't care what you think."

"Anyway," I said, desperately changing the subject. "I was telling Boges earlier about seeing that guy again, the one that looks like my double— "

"You saw someone who looked like your double?" Winter interrupted. Her expression had changed. She was frowning, worried.

I nodded. "This time I saw him coming out of the high school down the road."

I was puzzled at the way Winter's face had turned so pale and by the way she was staring at me. She seemed to know something I didn't.

"You OK? Why should *you* be so worried?" I continued. "I'm the crazy one seeing double!"

"Crazy is right!" Boges said, as he suddenly grabbed his school backpack. "Only someone who's totally crazy would share so much information with someone who has friends like Sligo." He swung around to face Winter Frey. "And as for you, you should back off and leave Cal alone!"

"I'm only trying to help him!" she said. "Don't be so quick to judge! You don't know the first thing about me!"

The two of them stared fiercely at each other.

"OK, calm down everyone," I said. "Boges, I can take care of myself. I'm a big boy. We need all the help we can get with this." I pointed to the Riddle on the table. "That's why we're all here — to solve this."

Boges made a snorting sound, while Winter nodded her head, agreeing with me.

"Cool. So let's have a look at the Riddle." I paused.

"The words just don't make any sense to me. What do you think?" I asked, turning to Winter.

Winter reached over Boges to take the Riddle. As she did so, I saw the tiny bird tattoo once more, on the inside of her wrist. It made me think of her locket and the "Little Bird" inscription on the back. Sure enough, the heart-shaped necklace dangled from her neck.

"Can't you see what she's trying to do?" said Boges. "She's going to take this information right back to Sligo, and then he'll know we've got it. He's already coming after you — he'll come after you a hundred times harder if he knows you've got the Riddle!"

"I've already explained how things are with me and Mr. Sligo. I'm not interested in helping him, and I don't agree with the way he lives his life." She sighed as she looked at me. "I'm not going to go over this again — your friend is determined to dislike me."

"Distrust is the word I'd use," Boges snapped.

"You guys better make up your minds. Do you want my help or not?"

Boges shrugged, as if he suddenly didn't care. I reached down, picked up the Riddle text again, and passed it to her.

Winter smiled sweetly, then studied the Riddle

text for a few moments in silence.

"Somebody's cut it." She pointed to the clean-cut edge at the bottom of the piece of vellum and then looked up at me, wanting an explanation.

"Yeah, the last two lines are missing," I said.

"That's going to make it extra hard — a lot of riddles are written with their solution in the final lines." She studied the words of the Riddle a little longer.

"This looks like a number riddle to me," she said, finally. "Look at all the numbers in it — eight, thirteen, one — and down here it even says 'adde One in.'"

I looked down at the flowery words. "Why are all the words spelled so strangely?" I asked.

"Spelling didn't have standard rules in the days this was written," she said.

"That's right," added Boges. "People could spell words however they liked."

"So do you think we're supposed to add all the numbers together or something?" I asked, doing the quick calculation. "Because if we are, the total is twenty-two."

"So we've got twenty-two," said Boges. "What help is that?" I could tell he still didn't really want to find anything Winter Frey said or did helpful.

"Boges," I said, "we've got to try everything. You said so yourself."

"That monkey drawing," said Winter, pointing at the picture on the floor. "He looks kind of familiar. I feel like I've seen him somewhere before."

"I suppose you'll take Cal to look at some memorial in a park now," said Boges. "A memorial for fallen monkeys."

I groaned, wishing this stupid bickering between them would stop, but to my surprise, Winter actually started laughing.

I looked over at Boges and could have sworn he was stifling a smile.

"These awesome drawings," she said, pointing to each one in turn, "you need to put some words in front of them."

"What do you mean?" I asked, very interested to hear what she was about to say.

"Think," she replied. "Remember the Angel drawing? And how I took you to the cenotaph, and there he was? It was like the drawing of the Angel was telling you something, telling you to look for . . ."

" . . . For an angel," I continued. Then I picked up the monkey drawing. "So I should be looking for a monkey? I should be looking for this kid with the flower?"

"This old Roman guy?" I added.

"Right," she said. "And you should be looking for a sphinx . . ." she paused, frowning, "or maybe that one was telling you about the Riddle."

I flashed a smug glance at Boges. Even he had to be impressed with that, I thought. She was picking up the connections fast.

"You know about the riddle of the Sphinx?" I asked.

"It's no secret," she said, "if you've studied ancient history or Greek drama. You should also be looking for a butler with a blackjack."

"A *butler*?" I said. "I've always thought of him as a waiter."

She shrugged. "He looks like a butler to me. Butler, waiter, whatever. You should be looking for all of those things."

"So why do you think the monkey's familiar?" I asked.

"I'm not sure, but I think it might be the collar, or the ball or something . . ."

Winter's phone started ringing.

"Back in a sec," she said, stepping away from us.

"Don't you see what she's doing?" Boges's voice was serious. "She's using us. Pretending to be friends with us, and all the time she's running off and telling everything to her criminal friends! That's what she's doing, and you're too blind to see it!"

"But Boges," I started to say, until Winter's angry voice cut me short. She was off the phone and had heard everything Boges had said.

"I've had enough of this! I'm not standing around here listening to this! I can't keep justifying myself, trying to make you trust me. It's been hard ignoring your snide comments, but you've gone too far!" I heard a catch in her voice. She sounded really hurt.

She snatched up her bag and flung it over her shoulder, her sparkling hair flying everywhere. "You're on your own, Cal Ormond! Obviously you have enough help here already. I even told you earlier that I had something really important to tell you, but it looks like you don't even care, so why should I? If you want to speak to me, Cal, you'll know where to find me."

"Wait! What did you have to tell me?"

She slipped through the door and hurried away, scrambling up the riverbank.

I ran outside after her, but she was too fast for me. She'd already vanished.

"Now look what you've done, Boges!" I said, exasperated, when I hurried back to the boathouse. "She was making progress, getting things really fast, and you've gone and driven her away!"

"Any fool could see that the Riddle had numbers in it! That's no big deal! She wasn't telling us anything new."

"Plus she made the connection between the Sphinx and the Riddle!"

We glared at each other. Boges and I rarely argued, and it didn't feel good at all. "We need all the help we can get," I said.

"You seriously want to bring her in on this investigation? Just because she's sucked you in by showing you the Angel at the cenotaph? And *pretending* she's got more information? Look at the facts, man! She's a member of a criminal gang who has already tried to wipe you out!"

There followed an angry silence, which Boges finally broke, shoving his face close to mine. "I don't care how *cute* she is, her friends have tried to kill you! What is it about attempted murder you don't understand?"

Both of us were really angry now. I was about to gather up the drawings and pack them away together with the Riddle, when I heard the sound of a car skidding to a halt up on the road.

"I'm going to go and find her," I said.

"You *are* crazy!" he said. "And you *will* be sorry! It sounds like her thugs are here already! I'm outta here," he said, before running out the door and disappearing.

Car doors slammed. My sixth sense warned me that they weren't picnickers.

Instead of going outside the door to look, where I could easily be seen, I braced myself and slipped into the water.

Trying not to splash too much, I waded through the boathouse doors and around the corner to check who it was that had skidded to a halt up there on the road.

When I saw the car parked at the top of the nature reserve, I freaked out!

It was the black Subaru! Vulkan's car!

My backpack! I wanted to swim around to get back in the boathouse, but realized I didn't have time — I needed to get away! Instead I swam to the shore, then scrambled along the riverbank and ran, stumbling past small, muddy beaches and other boat sheds, ducking under the piers of small jetties, leaving the black Subaru and its occupants on the hill behind me.

Boges's words were ringing in my ears. Why did I trust Winter? The last time I'd made my desperate dash — down into the railway tunnels — I'd just spoken to Winter Frey. Boges was smart. Maybe he was right about this. She seemed to bring the black Subaru hard on her heels.

My confusion grew. I wanted to find her and get to the bottom of this, once and for all. Had she given my location away, or had they tailed her?

She'd said I'd know where to find her. And I did.

Memorial Park
Cenotaph

1:07 pm

She was sitting underneath the Ormond Angel on one of the benches that ran around the perimeter.

I knew that's where she would go — where I would find her.

She didn't look up when I approached, like

she was waiting for me. She sat with her arms around her knees and her head resting on them, her wild hair hanging down, her shoulder bag on the ground beside her. I came up to her and stood near her, wondering what to say.

Slowly, she lifted her head, and I could see she'd been crying.

"Seems like whenever you're around, Sligo isn't far behind," I said.

"What are you talking about?"

"I just ran from them. The black Subaru turned up at the river just after you left."

She rolled her eyes. "It's nothing to do with me, I promise! It could have been Boges they followed! They've been watching his every movement, you know! I'm so careful, Cal. I don't want to put you in danger!"

My mind was telling me that it was definitely her that had turned me in, but my heart wouldn't believe it.

She lifted her head again and wiped her smudged eyes. "I'll tell you what I overheard, and maybe you'll understand how Sligo seems to find out where you are. Then maybe you'll finally trust me."

"I'm listening."

"OK," she said. "Yesterday when I was at

Sligo's place, Zombrovski had a meeting with this other guy. I'd just had a quick swim and had gone upstairs to change in the bathroom, when I heard them arguing outside by the back gate. I peeked through the blinds and saw that the other guy with the teardrop tattoo on his face— "

"Kelvin!"

"You know him?"

"We've had a few run-ins! He works for Oriana de la Force."

"That's who they were talking about! But I'd better start at the beginning. This Kelvin guy owes Zombrovski money, apparently. Some big gambling debt."

"Right," I said, "I already know they're both crooks. And that Kelvin's a gambler."

"I haven't finished yet," she said. "Kelvin's been struggling to repay it, so to avoid ending up dead in the bottom of the ocean, he told Zombrovski that Oriana de la Force has some way of— " she paused and looked around, making sure we were completely alone before repeating, "Oriana de la Force has some way of always knowing where you are."

A shiver of fear ran through me. "How could she possibly always know where I am? Half the time *I* don't even know where I am!"

"I'm just telling you what I heard. Kelvin was offering information as payment, instead of money. To settle his gambling debt."

I shook my head, thinking of all the times I'd been shocked that he and Sumo had been able to locate me.

"But how does she know where I am?" I repeated, recalling the first time I'd met Kelvin, during a beating outside the casino. "Is someone always spying on me? Tailing me?"

She shrugged with her usual impatience. "I don't know, he didn't say anything about how they knew, but that could explain how Sligo seems to just turn up no matter where you are. Pretty reliable information, it seems. Perhaps he's been handing it over for a while."

I didn't like the sound of this at all. I looked around, freaked out. Was someone watching me right now? The back of my neck prickled, as goose bumps rose. I swung around, but there was no one in the cenotaph except the two of us.

"I know Boges thinks it's because of me — that I pass your secrets on to Sligo . . . but he's wrong. Completely wrong. Kelvin is passing information from his boss, Oriana de la Force, on to Zombrovski, who then tells Sligo."

As much as I hated hearing this, I wanted to believe she was telling the truth.

"Kelvin also said something about the Ormond Riddle. It didn't make any sense to me at the time, and I couldn't understand exactly what he said, but then when I saw it at your place today, I remembered hearing it."

"What?" I asked.

"Like I said, it didn't make much sense to me then, and I might have gotten some of the words wrong, but I thought he said something about a double-key code."

"A double-key code? What does that mean?"

"I don't know. Maybe it's something to do with how you figure out the Riddle. Those numbers might have something to do with it." She looked around me, urgently. "Where's your backpack?" she asked. "Don't tell me you left it behind?"

My anxious face must have told her the answer to that.

She stood up, shaking out her purple skirt and picking up her bag. We both started walking away from the Ormond Angel, heading towards the rusty iron gates that led to the steps down from the cenotaph into the park.

"I guess the double-key code means what it says — that the code requires a double key — two keys — to solve it."

I sighed. "We haven't even gotten *one* yet.

"I need your help, Winter," I continued, as we stood at the top of the steps, "to solve the Riddle. I know you're mad at Boges, but I hope you can not let that worry you too much and concentrate on helping me solve this huge mystery. I've also got some letters that I need both of you to look at."

The black Subaru swung into the street near the entrance to Memorial Park.

I couldn't believe it! It was back again!

"Sligo!" she cried. "I can't let him see me with you!"

We looked around for another way out of the park, but I knew from past experience that there wasn't one. How were we going to get out of this?

I looked around desperately. I could see two figures getting out of the black Subaru — any moment now and they'd see me!

"Stay here. Don't move," Winter ordered, pushing me back into the interior of the cenotaph building. "Just stay put. Don't let them see you. Leave this to me!"

With a swirl of her purple skirt, she ran down the steps and along the path.

When I thought it was safe, I carefully poked my head around the gates to find Winter standing in deep conversation with Bruno and Zombrovski, neither of whom was looking in my direction. The three of them continued to stand in conversation a few moments longer, then Winter climbed into the back seat of the car, the other two in the front, and the Subaru did a noisy three-point turn and disappeared.

I slumped with relief. Somehow she'd deflected them. Had she put them on a false trail? What had she said?

I had to get back to the boathouse and pick up my backpack. I hoped with everything I had that it would still be there. The sick feeling in my stomach told me otherwise.

I took off, anger and confusion making my heart pound almost in time with my flying feet.

I skidded to a halt at the corner, checking out the street. I couldn't see the black Subaru anywhere — but Sligo, with his connection to a car lot, could have any amount of cars available.

Head down, trying to look invisible, I made my way back to the boathouse, walking whenever I saw people looking at me, running at other times.

I hated the thought of Oriana de la Force always knowing where I was. I kept looking around, trying to spot whomever it might have been that was tailing me for her. It seemed impossible that she could keep track of my movements. I looked around with suspicion. *Is it you?* I asked, with every passing person. *Or you?*

The boathouse
Greenaway Park

2:23 pm

I raced down through the nature reserve and into the boathouse.

I stopped in my tracks and cried out as I saw the old door off its hinges. The boathouse had been trashed! My backpack had been upended and was lying on the floor. My clothes were scattered all over the room. I raced over to my crumpled bag, but I could tell just from looking at it that the drawings and the Riddle were gone!

Bruno and Zombrovski had been through my stuff! Before I even had a chance to find out what was missing, someone grabbed me from behind. I felt a piercing pain in my neck, and then I slumped.

3:56 pm

Confusion and chaos whirled around me. I felt like I was flying through darkness. Then I was falling into a black pit.

Strange sounds filled my ears.

Crying, wailing, people calling out in strange languages. I tried to move and found I couldn't.

I sank back down into the darkness.

30 APRIL

246 days to go . . .

11:12 pm

My eyes flew open. I looked around. I was in a strange bed. The room was all white — the walls and ceiling, even the curtains that hung at the window. I struggled to move and found that my arms seemed to be in some sort of coat that restrained my movements. I tried to remember what had happened. I recalled seeing Winter in the park and talking about the double-key code, then going back to the boathouse to get my bag. The last thing I remembered was making it to the boathouse and realizing that the drawings and the Ormond Riddle were gone.

A pain in my neck reminded me of the stinging sensation I'd felt there, just before everything went hazy into blackness.

Someone must have grabbed me silently from behind and stabbed me in the neck with one of my own tranquilizer darts.

I didn't know how long I'd been in this nightmare state. Freaky visions filled the space behind my closed eyes, my ears filled with horrible shrieks. I had no idea where I was. I could feel the sweat of fear breaking out all over my body, because the sounds around me were starting to take shape. The cries, the wailing voices, the sobs — all those strange noises I'd heard while I'd been in some sort of sedated nightmare, were now becoming much clearer.

I was in some house where all around me the other rooms were filled with haunted people. Why were they crying like that? Was this some sort of prison? Again, I struggled to free my arms, but whatever was restraining them didn't budge. I looked down to see that I'd been dressed in what looked like a shirt that was on back to front. With some relief, I found that my feet were free, so I kicked the covers back and got out of the bed, wobbling a bit until I found my balance.

I hurried to the window and looked out past strong iron bars to see that I was on the second floor of a sandstone building, erected around a bare quadrangle. Three people in long white nightshirts shuffled along the central path. I stumbled over to the door, and although there was no way I could have opened it, something told me it was locked.

Some blurry gray lettering on the bed sheets started becoming clearer.

Then I saw that there was a chart at the end of my bed, and I went over to look at it.

PATIENT CHART

Patient:	Ben Galloway
Admission date:	29 April
Admitting Physician:	Dr Elliot Porter
Psychiatrist:	Dr Alistair Snudgeglasser

Diagnosis: Acute paranoia and delusions

R/x: 5mls i/v Sedatonin 6 hourly

CAUTION: HDP: Must not be moved without Level 5 Restraints.

Leechwood Lodge ASYLUM

Slowly, I started to make sense of what had happened. Someone had created a new, completely false identity for me and had me admitted to this nuthouse as Ben Galloway. Whoever this Dr. Elliot Porter was, he'd either been duped by false documents, or was part of the conspiracy to lock me up in here. In the fine print at the bottom, I saw where I was: Leechwood Lodge Asylum.

I'd heard of this place over the years — Leechwood Lodge. The kids used to call it the Crazy House. Where the mad, bad and dangerous were locked away.

I stared at the hospital chart with disbelief. Then rage. Somehow I had been set up and admitted! I went to the door and kicked it as hard as I could with my bare feet.

"Let me out of here!" I yelled. "I'm not Ben Galloway! You've got it all wrong! I need to speak to someone!"

Nobody came. But my voice had stirred up the other inmates, and their yells and howls echoed mine, up and down the corridor outside my locked door.

I slumped against the bed, despairing. This was a terrible place, and nobody knew where I was. How could they? I didn't know where

Boges was — whether he'd gotten away from the boathouse, or whether he'd been grabbed from the road . . . Who knows what Sligo was capable of doing! Or Oriana de la Force!

I looked around the room to see that none of my possessions were there. No clothing. No sneakers. There wasn't even a chair or a table. The walls were bare except for a list of fire regulations and drills. My phone was gone. I had nothing except this straitjacket that made my arms and hands useless, and the white hospital nightshirt that hung down almost to my ankles.

I had to get out! Sligo's thugs must have stolen the drawings and the Ormond Riddle and taken them straight to him. It sounded like he already knew about the double-key code, thanks to Oriana's rat, Kelvin. What if they solved the Riddle?! Sligo could do it easily with Winter's help.

Winter! In the hazy state I was in I was convinced that she'd fooled me, and that I'd fallen for her act. How could I have been so stupid? Just because she'd shown me her soft side a couple of times. I was furious with her and furious with myself. I should have listened to Boges. Not only had she probably betrayed me to Sligo, but she had enabled the drawings and the Riddle to fall into his hands. She'd tricked me into trusting her. She'd set me up like a total sucker. She was a thief and a traitor, and at that moment, I hated her.

And Boges must have been angry with me too. I'd lost everything connected to my dad's secret and put him in danger.

How was I going to escape from Leechwood Lodge? I had to get out, find the Ormond Riddle and my dad's drawings, go to Mount Helicon. My family needed me. I had to escape!

This time, I ran hard at the door, banging it with my body weight, yelling at the top of my voice, "Somebody! I need to talk to somebody! There's been a big mistake!"

This time I heard heavy footsteps clattering down the corridor. Someone unlocked the door.

"Please!" I said, as two heavy-built men wearing hospital greens charged into my room. "There's been a big mistake," I repeated. "I shouldn't be in here. My name isn't Ben Galloway! You need to let me out!"

Neither of the big hospital orderlies spoke. Instead, they lifted me back onto the bed and tied me, feet too, to the bed, with wide white straps, so that I couldn't move at all.

"I've got to talk to someone! Please! I need to see the doctor! I need to see the person in charge of this place! I'm not Ben Galloway!"

The two orderlies walked out without a word, slamming and locking the door behind them.

I lay on the bed, screaming.

The door opened, and the tallest of the orderlies stood there, a nasty smile on his face.

"We can give you twenty mLs of Dormadoze, and you'll be out for a week, or you can quiet down. It's up to you."

"Everybody screams in here," the shorter one added. "No one pays any attention. You'll get sick of it soon enough." He started backing out, closing the heavy door. "They all do in time."

I heard him locking the door, and then heard his final muffled words. "You can scream all you like, kid. Goodnight."

45 RACE AGAINST TIME 06:48 07:12 05:21 RACE AGAI
ICE AGAINST TIME SEEK THE TRUTH . . . CONSPIRACY 3
IE SOMETHING IS SERIOUSLY MESSED UP HERE 08:30
:06 06:07 APRIL WHO CAN CAL TRUST? SEEK THE TR
:04 10:08 RACE AGAINST TIME 02:27 08:06 10:32 SEE
IE TRUTH 01:00 07:57 SOMETHING IS SERIOUSLY MES
:01 09:53 CONSPIRACY 365 12:00 RACE AGAINST TIM
RIL WHO CAN CAL TRUST? 01:09 LET THE COUNTDOW
RIL HIDING SOMETHING? 03:32 01:47 05:03 APRIL LE
UNTDOWN BEGIN 09:06 10:33 11:45 RACE AGAINST TIM
:12 05:21 RACE AGAINST TIME RACE AGAINST TIME SE
UTH . . . CONSPIRACY 365 TRUST NO ONE 06:07 SOME
RIOUSLY MESSED UP HERE 08:30 12:01 05:07 06:06 0
IO CAN CAL TRUST? SEEK THE TRUTH 12:05 APRIL 06
ICE AGAINST TIME 02:27 08:06 10:32 SEEK THE TRUT
METHING IS SERIOUSLY MESSED UP HERE 05:01 09:5
NSPIRACY 365 12:00 RACE AGAINST TIME 04:31 10:17
N CAL TRUST? 01:09 LET THE COUNTDOWN BEGIN AP
METHING? 03:32 01:47 05:03 APRIL LET THE COUNTI
:06 10:33 11:45 RACE AGAINST TIME 06:48 07:12 05:2
AINST TIME RACE AGAINST TIME SEEK THE TRUTH . .
S TRUST NO ONE SOMETHING IS 06:07 SERIOUSLY MI
RE 08:30 12:01 05:07 06:06 06:07 APRIL WHO CAN CA
EK THE TRUTH 12:05 APRIL 06:04 10:08 RACE AGAINS
:27 08:06 10:32 SEEK THE TRUTH 01:00 07:57 SOMET
RIOUSLY MESSED UP HERE 05:01 09:53 CONSPIRACY
CE AGAINST TIME 04:31 10:17 APRIL WHO CAN CAL TR
T THE COUNTDOWN BEGIN APRIL HIDING SOMETHING?
47 05:03 APRIL LET THE COUNTDOWN BEGIN 09:06 1
CE AGAINST TIME 06:48 07:12 05:21 RACE AGAINST T
AINST TIME SEEK THE TRUTH . . . CONSPIRACY 365 TI
METHING IS 06:07 SERIOUSLY MESSED UP HERE 08:
:07 06:06 06:07 APRIL WHO CAN CAL TRUST? SEEK T
05 APRIL 06:04 10:08 RACE AGAINST TIME 02:27 08:
EK THE TRUTH 01:00 07:57 SOMETHING IS SERIOUSLY